THE SCARRED PRINCE

TALES FROM THE KINGDOMS OF FABLE
BOOK 1

ERIKA EVEREST

THE SCARRED PRINCE (this book) is a work of fiction.
All of the characters and events portrayed in this novel are fictitious.
Similarities to real people, places, or events are coincidental.

Cover by Andrew Dobell www.creativeedgestudios.co.uk

First Edition published October 2020 (v1.0)

ISBN-13 (ebook): 978-1-913972-01-1

ISBN-13 (print): 978-1-913972-02-8

Created with Vellum

For Dad,
This isn't the book we said we would write together,
But I know you would have been proud anyway.

Jitterbugs Beta Team

Arielle Bailey
James Caplan
Micky Cocker
Dorothy Lloyd
Angela Marshall
Kelly O'Donnell
Natale Roberts
Robyn Sarty
Coralie Terry
Laura Wainscott
Sarah Weir

MAP OF FABLE

Fable
Northern Ocean
Eddally
Sea of Eddally
Karjala
Anglia
500 miles
Bay of Anglia
Karjalan Straight
Bretonnia
Hessenburg
Northaven
Siverus
Vitalia
Clodonia
Herzvorak
Cadiza
Orella
Oreilan Sea
Mythika
Gulf of Mythika
Fokklor
© Erika Everest

1

There was a girl in his private study.

His *locked* private study.

How the blazes had she gotten in? This was meant to be his retreat, the one place he could drop the mask and be himself. He pulled the hood of his red cloak further forward to be sure it hid his face.

"Who are you?" he demanded.

"I'm your newest recruit for the Rangers," she said with a cheerful smile, as if this was perfectly normal.

"But you're a woman."

"With such heightened deductive skills, I can see why you are considered the leading Intelligence Officer in Fable." It took him a moment to realize she was mocking him because *no one* ever dared to mock him. He was Prince Sebastian, first heir to his brother King Philippe of Vitalia and Commander of the King's Army. He was the conqueror of cities and defender of the realm, known to both his enemies and his allies as the Wolf of the West. He scrutinized her, this intruder who showed neither deference nor fear toward him. She couldn't be more than sixteen or seventeen. She was of medium height and average build, but that was the only average thing about her. Even with her hair pulled back, and no make-up or jewelry or the other adornments ladies usually wore to increase their attractiveness, she could only be described as beautiful. In fact, beautiful seemed too ordinary a word. She was the most stunningly pretty girl he had ever seen. She wore a plain but well-made blue dress, which complemented her honey-toned skin and brought out the chestnut highlights in her hair. There was a joyful innocence about her that was at odds with her stated desire to join the most elite company of soldiers and spies on the continent. But when he looked more closely, he saw the hard glint of steel in her gaze. She probably would fit in well with his Rangers except for the fact that she was, well, a woman.

"How did you get in here?"

"Through the door, obviously." She gave him a sly smile. "You really should be careful about who you trust with your keys."

That threw him for a moment. The only people who had keys to his rooms in the castle were... no, he refused to believe they would have betrayed him like that. "No one on my staff would have let you in here," he said confidently.

"It wasn't one of the castle staff."

"My Rangers are even less likely to betray me," he said coldly.

"True," she agreed with that same cheerfulness. "But you have forgotten someone. You see, I've heard the stories about you. You haven't been seen outside this castle since you called off your engagement four years ago unless the King mandates your appearance at Court, and the only people who are admitted to the castle are your staff, Rangers, and family. There's even royalty who have been denied entry! So I knew I would have to do something drastic to get admitted and gain your attention. I did my research on you, and on this place. After all 'The prepared mind is better equipped to face the challenges that may come his way. Opportunities may go unrecognized by the less studious, as he has no context in which to assess the possibilities. But the mind that studies his opponents and the terrain in advance will have the advantage at the moment when fate presents an opening, for he will have the knowledge to see it and seize it.'"

"That's from *The Strategic Soldier*," he said, his surprise evident. "You read my book?"

"Actually, I've read all of your books."

"And you remember passages verbatim?"

"I may have read them more than once..." She trailed off, almost as if she was embarrassed to admit to it. Sebastian was caught off guard. Certainly, he had not expected the angel-faced child in front of him to have read his long and admittedly dry treatises on military strategy and training. It made him consider that perhaps there was more to her than just a pretty face.

"What's your name?" he asked, realizing that he had skipped this basic courtesy.

"Carissa Nicoletta Antonella."

"Right, Carissa –"

"Oh no, don't call me that. Only my father calls me Carissa."

"So what should I call you?" he huffed, exasperated.

"Most people call me by my initials – C N A, Sienna. You can call me that too."

"Fine, Sienna then. You were telling me how you got into this locked room deep inside my castle?"

"So, a little under twenty-five years ago, during your father's reign, there was a fire in this castle. Within two years, the reconstruction work was completed. Now, there is no public record of the company you used for the construction work, so I had to do a little digging. I started with the assumption that you would not use foreign companies to repair a Vitalian royal residence, and then looked at the financial status of the main construction companies within Vitalia. Within six months of the completion of the reconstruction, Hamm and Sons had dramatically increased in size, suggesting an influx of capital that would coincide with the final payments for the repairs.

"So I had a likely target and did my research on them. Did you know that Hamm and Sons have fifty-six different lock-and-key designs? I wasn't sure how I could narrow that down – if I even had the right company – but I had a little luck on my side. Hervé Hamm, or Hamm Senior as he seems to be more generally known, is the founder of the business and was the brains behind it. But his mind has been failing these past few years, which is when he handed over the running of the company to his three grandsons – hence the name change to Hamm Bros. Construction. The innkeeper in town is very knowledgeable about the family and was happy to share some harmless gossip with a curious stranger who admired the town's architecture. He also told me that Diego runs the business now, and is generally nicknamed 'Shrewd Hamm,' Carlos is a rake who likes to think of himself as 'Sexy Hamm' but is called 'Smarmy Hamm' behind his back by most people, and Auguste, the third brother is the biggest of them all but has a mind like a child. The townsfolk call him 'Slow Hamm,' or sometimes 'Sturdy Hamm' if they are being kinder. His brothers are protective of him, so have set him up as the primary carer for Hamm Senior, so that neither are exposed much to outsiders who might be cruel to them."

"While your description of people I have known most of my life is *riveting*," Sebastian interrupted, sarcasm oozing from every word, "Could you please get to the point of this rambling story?"

"I decided to pay Slow Hamm a visit. He was delighted to have someone to talk to him, and show interest in what he had to say, and was very forthcoming because of it. He confirmed that the Hamms had done the reconstruction on the castle within a few minutes of meeting me. So I probed about how they managed to keep all the different designs straight, and he confided that because Senior's memory is not what it was, they have to keep notes of which lock design has been used in each location, and that's Slow's job. He even makes little model boxes to help his grandfather remember his past achievements. They're very good – I was able to find my way to this door with no problems – and every door on the model has a number to identify the lock design. Then Slow showed me the display case of locks and keys, each helpfully labeled with the corresponding number. It was easy enough to lift the relevant key – number 23, by the way – and press it into a block of wax I had with me for that purpose while Slow made tea for his grandfather and the two of us. Senior is charming and seemed as delighted as Slow to have some outside company. After half an hour I thanked them for their hospitality and took my leave.

"Back in the inn that night, I melted down a spoon and poured the molten metal into the wax mold to make my own key 23. Then it was just a matter of watching the castle for a few days to learn the guard rotations to find a good time to slip by and make my way to your study to wait for you. And so here I am."

"Here you are," Sebastian repeated. Begrudgingly, he admired her. Her tactical planning was well thought out and well-executed. Not many people would have the audacity to break into a Prince's home. He certainly hadn't expected it from a little girl! But tactics and tenacity aside, there was no way a woman was cut out to be a Ranger. Yet he felt it would be callous to disregard her efforts so far with a flat-out dismissal. He smiled evilly as an idea occurred to him.

"Very well Sienna, you have impressed me. You can be a Ranger recruit. *If* you can pass the initiation test."

"What sort of test?"

"Trial by combat."

Her eyes widened. "Okay," she said hesitantly. "Who will I be competing against and when?"

"Sir Marcus de Meilleu, tomorrow at noon." He was gratified to see her blanch at the name. Sir Marcus was the Captain of the Rangers, and the only better swordsman in Vitalia was Sebastian himself. He was also Sebastian's best friend since childhood. "You can pick the weapons if you like," Sebastian offered magnanimously. The outcome was assured, but he could at least give her the illusion of a chance. She gulped but drew herself together. Sebastian could see the determination filling her and knew what her answer would be before she spoke.

"I accept your terms."

"Wonderful." Sebastian pulled the bell to summon the housekeeper. "Well, you better get across to the barracks to get settled then, so you can be rested for your trial tomorrow. Where is your luggage?"

Sienna pointed to a small knapsack by the wall.

"That's all you brought?" Sebastian asked in surprise. Either she had been far less certain of her success than she was projecting, or she was the rarest of creatures – a woman who could travel for a few weeks without needing a convoy of carriages to transport her possessions.

"Don't carry into battle anything you would regret to leave behind," she replied simply. He was taken aback by her quotation from his books again. Obviously, she had taken his words more deeply to heart than he had realized.

A quick rap on the door preceded the arrival of a plump and kindly-looking woman. "Ah, Mrs. Chambers, thank you. This is Sienna. She is the newest recruit for the Rangers."

"But she's a woman," his housekeeper said, stunned. Behind him, he heard a snort that he chose to ignore.

"Even so, she is a Rangers recruit. So can you please show her to the Barracks and introduce her to Master Joshua to get her quarters set up?"

"But sir, *she's a woman*. You can't let a young lady in amongst the soldiers. As for sleeping there, well! That just wouldn't be proper. She'll just have to sleep here in the castle. Come on, Miss Sienna," she said, looking past the Prince. "I'll have a room set up for you in no time. I'll put you in the Blue Suite." She bustled out of the study and Sienna followed in her wake. Sebastian was only slightly mollified by the glance she gave him as she left, as if checking it was acceptable to follow the housekeeper's lead. Finally alone in his study, he discarded his hooded cloak and sat in his thinking chair by the fireplace.

"Let's see what you are really made of, Sienna."

2

"Is it true?"

Sir Marcus' shout from the other end of the corridor made Sebastian stop. He walked briskly toward his prince, the red hooded cloak that gave the Rangers their nickname billowing behind him. "Did you agree to allow a woman into my Rangers?"

"My Rangers," Sebastian corrected automatically; it was an old joke between them. "Of course not. The Rangers is no place for a woman."

"Then what is *she* doing in my practice room?"

"She put some effort into getting here and getting my attention. I told her that she could try-out. That way we can get rid of her quickly without lots of female hysterics."

"What's the try-out?"

"You duel with her. She can pick the weapon and she has to win to stay. So wrap it up quickly, please. I want to get on with more serious training."

"Yes sir!" Marcus saluted with a grin. He fell into step beside Sebastian and headed for the training room. He was curious to see the woman who had managed to convince the taciturn prince to allow her a chance to prove herself, however futile. Marcus was taken aback somewhat when he entered the room. The young girl was not what he had been expecting. A female fighter... he had pictured an older, stouter woman. Not this beautiful girl who looked like a strong wind might knock her over. She was standing with her back to them when they entered, evaluating the different weapons that lined the walls of the room. She started when she realized that they were there, and hastily dropped a curtsey toward them.

"Shall we begin?" Sebastian asked, clearly ready for this ordeal to be over and done with.

"Any weapon?" Sienna asked, staring around at the vast array lining the walls of the practice room. Sebastian nodded. She had already been down here looking around since breakfast finished, so he figured she already had a good idea of what she wanted to use.

"Any weapon you chose and if you can beat Marcus then I'll train you as a Ranger." Sienna went to the wall and, after a moment's hesitation, picked a sword. Marcus and Sebastian shared a small smile; they both knew how unlikely it was that she could beat him with a sword.

Sebastian looked at Marcus' lazy, confident smile as he took another sword off the wall and almost felt sorry for the girl. Marcus started warming up, feinting at her. Sebastian noted that she did have a good grip on the sword handle, and seemed to have a good feel for its weight and balance. She darted back out of the way of Marcus' blade, compensating for his longer reach by being quicker and lighter on her feet. She continued to dodge, which started to frustrate the captain; he dropped the bored demeanor and committed to the bout.

Sebastian was used to Marcus toying with lesser opponents, giving them a supposed opening only to bat them aside easily, but something seemed off. He wasn't responding quickly enough to those feints, and Sienna was getting through his guard. His sword was dropping lower, as if he was having difficulty holding it. The strain showed on his face until he couldn't fight it anymore. He dropped his guard and Sienna darted in, grazing his hand lightly to draw blood.

"First blood," she claimed, stepping back.

Marcus dropped his sword completely and clutched his sword arm with his other hand.

"My arm! I can't feel it!" he cried in alarm.

"What is this?" Sebastian demanded of Sienna, as she didn't seem in any way surprised at the complete failure of the second-best swordsman in the kingdom against an untrained novice.

"You said I could use any weapon I wanted," Sienna replied. "You assumed I chose swords, but I never said that. The weapon I chose was poison."

Both men stared at her in fascinated horror.

"You poisoned me?"

"What have you done to him? Can you fix it?"

Two voices, incredulous and outraged, overlapped as they broke the moment of stunned silence together.

"Don't worry, it's not permanent," Sienna hastened to reassure them. "It's called silver nutmeg, a spice the eastern traders use. There, women use it when their husbands demand um, marital duties, that they don't want to perform; a little silver nutmeg stops the husbands from um, being in the mood."

"You've made me impotent?"

"No, you have to ingest it for that and I just put it on the sword hilts. But the effects are temporary anyway. Here, I brought the antidote with me. I've already used this. If you rub this on your hand should feel better soon."

Marcus grunted and took the antidote from her. He had difficulty trying to hold the small pot while simultaneously rubbing the cream onto his numb arm but eventually he got his whole arm covered. He looked at it, waiting for something to happen.

"It will take a few moments to take effect," Sienna told him.

"Choosing poison as a weapon is hardly a good way to improve your sword fighting skills," said Sebastian with a frown.

"No, but perhaps this is a good way to convince you that I am worth training," Sienna replied.

SHE STARED at the shadowed space where his eyes should be, and let him see the challenge in hers. They stared at each other as the moment stretched. With a muttered curse, Sebastian looked away first. A small victorious smile flitted across Sienna's face when he turned his back before she realized that Sir Marcus was watching their interaction intently. She schooled her expression again, hoping he hadn't seen it.

"Fine," Sebastian conceded grudgingly. "You fulfilled the terms of our deal so I will train you as a Ranger." He was too dignified to stomp out of the room, yet still managed to convey that impression as he left, Marcus trailing behind him.

Alone, Sienna slumped to the floor, her legs no longer able to support her as the adrenaline left her body in a rush. She was a little stunned that she had bluffed enough bravado to answer back to him. She had done it, she passed the test and was going to train with the Wolf himself! Now she just needed to prove to him that she was worth the chance she had been given.

~

SIENNA HESITATED in the doorway of the dining hall. Prince Sebastian was sitting at the head of the table, his face obscured by his hood as usual. She wondered if there was still time to slip away, plead a headache, and take supper in her room. She knew it was cowardly, but she wasn't sure what her reception would be after the stunt she pulled earlier with the silver nutmeg.

"Don't hover there, it's annoying. Come in, sit, eat."

The rich baritone voice sounded exasperated, so she hurried to comply. She still wasn't sure what his attitude toward her would be. If only she could see his face to give her a clue! Though, she admitted ruefully to herself, he probably had a wonderful poker face under there anyway; you don't get to the levels he reached by being easily read by others. She decided silence might be the safest course, so sat demurely and reached for a bread roll. It was still warm and broke apart easily in her hands. She looked for olive oil to drizzle on the bread, but seeing none she took a bite of it dry. It was so light it almost dissolved on her tongue. She savored it while surveying the dishes arrayed before her. The Prince was eating a soup that was such a deep red it was almost purple, but she bypassed the soup in favor of the duck confit and helped herself to the gratin dauphinoise and some of the vast selection of vegetable accompaniments. It seemed like a lot of food for just two people, but there didn't seem to be anyone else joining them. The Prince didn't say anything more to her once she was seated. He seemed absorbed in the letters and ledgers he was reading, and content to ignore her.

I didn't go through everything I did to get here to be frozen out now, she thought indignantly. 'Demure' was the girl who was afraid to stand up to her father for what she wanted, who shied away from confrontation. That girl was gone, Sienna would make sure of it. Not all battles were fought with weapons. She knew she was poking the bear – or the wolf – but she was determined to draw the Prince out and force him to engage with her. Silence might be safer, but she didn't come all this way to play it safe!

"Your castle is lovely. The views of the ocean are breathtaking."

No response.

"This seems like a lot of food for just two people. Will anyone else be joining us?"

More silence.

"I have a tendency to sleepwalk nude. That won't be a problem, will it?"

The Prince choked on his soup. He took a gulp of his wine and stared right at her once his coughing subsided.

"Oh good," Sienna said sweetly. "You *are* listening."

"You keep surprising me. Marcus too."

Sienna wasn't sure if his muttered comment was meant as a compliment or not, but he put his papers aside so she pushed on.

"How *is* Sir Marcus?" she asked tentatively, now that he had introduced the topic.

"No lasting damage except to his pride. And his pride is big enough that it can take the hits," Sebastian chortled in amusement. Sienna was taken aback slightly by his levity. From his books, she had thought him to be stern and staid, and certainly his behavior toward her so far had done nothing to disabuse her of that notion. She offered a small smile in return, delighted to have the opportunity to interact with the man she had idolized since she first discovered *A Memoir of Marching* nearly four years ago.

"That's a relief. I was afraid he might refuse to train me because of it."

"Then why do it?"

"Because you said you wouldn't let me stay unless I could beat him, and it was the only way I would have any chance against someone of his skill. I couldn't be sent away without learning how to defend myself, I just couldn't!"

THE FERVOR in her voice bordered on desperation, and it piqued Sebastian's curiosity. It seemed so at odds with the cheerful, confident girl who had broken into his sanctuary the night before.

"Why is this so important to you?" he asked. He watched her carefully via her reflection in one of the serving dishes, having long since learned to compensate for the reduction in his peripheral vision caused by his hood. She was silent for so long he thought she wasn't going to answer, but then she looked up. He wondered if the glazed look in her eyes was just a distortion caused by the curvature of the reflective surface.

"A few years ago, something bad happened to me. I was kidnapped with some other girls and ... well, I don't want to talk about what happened to us. We were lucky, we escaped. But I promised myself I would never be vulnerable like that again. I begged my father to teach me to fight but he refused. His idea for ensuring my safety was to find me a husband who could protect me, which still left me personally defenseless. So I trained myself in secret. But there is only so much you can learn swinging a sword at air, practicing moves designed for men twice your size. I knew I needed a real teacher, so I came to the best."

"You're married?" Sebastian didn't hide the surprise in his voice.

"Betrothed. And only technically," she hastened to add. "It's not like I had a say in the decision."

"I understand that it is frustrating that you were not consulted, but surely your fiancé isn't that bad, even if you didn't get to choose him?"

Sienna gave an inelegant snort. "He is an arrogant, insufferable jerk, and my inferior socially."

Her answer surprised Sebastian. "Is rank important to you?" he asked. He hadn't gotten that impression from her, given how little weight *his* rank seemed to carry with her.

"Not at all, but it is to him. On the one hand, he is delighted to be 'marrying up,' but at the same time, he cannot bear the fact that I outrank him. He deals with this by belittling me at every opportunity, treating me as a brainless damsel in distress, to bolster his own self-esteem. I couldn't face that future, so I ran away and came here to forge my own path and follow my dreams, instead of accepting my father's."

"You ran away? So no one knows you're here?"

"No, and I don't want them to. They'd only try to bring me back and push the wedding through sooner. I deliberately left while on the journey back to boarding school, to create a window where my absence won't be immediately missed. I want to stay undetected until I can prove to my father I don't need a husband to protect me, or I can find some other way out of the marriage."

"Where are you from, Sienna?"

She narrowed her eyes and looked at him shrewdly. "You wouldn't be thinking of finding my family and informing them of my whereabouts, would you?"

"Of course not," Sebastian lied. It was exactly what he had been thinking. She gave a little snort of disbelief.

"I grew up in Cadia," she told him. As the capital city of the neighboring kingdom of Cadiza, Cadia was hardly a small area, so her answer didn't tell him much. Sebastian understood her deliberate vagueness; she wasn't sure if she could trust him yet. But he had her family name as well as a location, and there was a lot he could do with that. Now that he had agreed to let her stay, Sebastian felt a responsibility toward her. She was younger than his own sister Eva and had no one looking out for her. Well, he could change that, starting now. It would take a couple of weeks for the school to realize she wasn't re-enrolling and contact the parents, who would then know she hadn't arrived and start a search for her. He had Rangers all over the continent; he would ask his intelligence agents in Cadia to keep an ear out for an Antonella family with a daughter in boarding school or any stories of a family in the city with a missing daughter. At that point, he could decide how to proceed, but for now, he would let her keep her secrets and not pry.

"So, what are you working on?" she asked, pointing at his papers as a change of topic.

"I commissioned a survey of the recent housing development in the Bourgeois Quarter, and the results are concerning. Many of the new buildings are being built of timber, because Hamm Bros. Construction won't pay to haul stone in from the quarries outside the city limits. That wouldn't be such a problem but the bakery and blacksmith's forge are in the same development – fire and timber do not make for happy homes. I'll have to issue a demolition notice to tear down those houses, which will be the second one I've issued for that company. The eco-homes were a nightmare!"

"I remember hearing about that. Houses built from dried grasses woven together with thatched roofs – "Be at one with your environment. Let nature into your home," or something like that, was the slogan, wasn't it?"

"Well, they very literally let nature into those homes. The straw quickly attracted mice, and then when the winter rains came it got so wet that mold and rot set in. The Hamms promised never to use such unsuitable building materials again, and yet here we are less than a year later in similar circumstances. But they are fighting me on it this time. They've said publicly that if the Schues in the Hessenberg Mountains can be made of timber then so can houses in Vitalia. It doesn't matter about the safety concerns. I huff and I puff until I'm blue in the face, but they're not listening. So I've been checking their financial records and discovered that they've invested so heavily in timber that they *can't* let their wooden houses go."

"How do you find time for keeping up with all of this?"

"You asked earlier if anyone else would be joining us for dinner, but the truth is I usually eat alone and catch up on my paperwork and correspondence."

"Isn't that awfully lonely?"

"It's very efficient; there really aren't enough hours in the day to get through it all otherwise."

"Oh," Sienna said, reddening. "I'm keeping you from your work with my chatter. I'll retire and let you continue."

"No, there is no need to leave," Sebastian reassured her, oddly unwilling to let her go.

"Well, it is late anyway. I should get some rest if I have to face Sir Marcus in the practice ring in the morning. Goodnight, Your Highness." She bobbed a half-curtsey then hurried from the room. The dining hall felt darker for her absence, so Sebastian decided to take his papers to his study instead. On the way, he pondered her question.

"Isn't that awfully lonely?"

He had never thought so before, but one evening of conversation and companionship from a stranger showed him a glimpse of the life he might be missing. How would it feel to have someone to share his table every mealtime, to ask about his day, and to offer new insights? To celebrate his successes and comfort in his failures? Perhaps he *had* been too hasty to shut out the world. Surely not every woman was like Lacey. The right woman for him was out there somewhere; he just had to find her.

"It's time I looked for a wife."

3

Sebastian's perusal of his papers was interrupted some time later by a gentle chime. He searched around the room frantically for his cloak and spied it tossed in the corner by the door. The chime became louder as a ripple shimmered across the surface of the mirror by his desk. There were only two people who could call him using that magic mirror: his sister and his brother. Given the late hour, he thought it was more likely to be Eva than Philippe. Sebastian had mixed feelings about magic. It certainly offered conveniences for those who could afford them but, in his experience, magic was too often in the hands of people willing to misuse it.

He pulled the cloak around him and picked up the mirror, swiping the surface just as the chime rose to an annoying pitch. As expected, it was Princess Eva's face he saw when he looked in the mirror.

"Hello Fairest," he greeted her.

"Hello Bravest," she replied, using the nicknames that their mother had coined and then used as their call signs when she had the magic mirrors commissioned so her children could communicate no matter how far apart they were. "Did I wake you?"

"No, I was just reading my correspondence."

"Then why did it take you so long to answer the mirror?"

"I wasn't wearing my hood," Sebastian explained. "I had to get it before I could answer."

"Oh Seb," Eva sighed. "You don't have to hide from me. I've seen your scars before."

"Well that's no reason for you to have to see them now," Sebastian huffed defensively. "And no reason I should have to look at them when this call ends and I'm holding a mirror again."

Eva looked like she would argue further, but she bit her lip and stayed quiet. There was nothing to say that hadn't been said before.

"So, any news from that drafty bastion of isolation that you call a home?"

"Evie, you know perfectly well that this castle is neither draughty nor isolated. As it happens, I do have news. I've decided it's time I got married." There was a shocked silence followed by a squeal of delight from Eva.

"Oh my gosh, are you serious? This is wonderful news! Who is she?"

"Slow down," Sebastian laughed at Eva's enthusiasm. "I don't have any immediate plans to head for the altar. I just realized I want that to be part of my future so I need to look for a bride again."

"That's great, Sebastian, really. Philippe and I had all but given up on you. We thought you were going to be the eternal bachelor. After what Lacey did, well..."

Princess Lacey: blonde hair, blue eyes, pouty lips. Granddaughter to the King of Karjala, and Sebastian's ex-fiancée. It had seemed like the perfect match. She was gorgeous and the darling of Society; he was the military hero, the dashing soldier. He was delighted to have the beauty by his side and while she didn't understand what he did as King's Commander, she was proud of his achievements. They were the golden couple of Fable, until the day a scorned and jealous witch cursed him. Scars ravaged the left side of his face, while the right side remained unblemished – a cruel twist so that he would never forget what had been taken from him. The best healers from all over Fable could do nothing to reverse the magically-inflicted wounds.

And Lacey, shallow coward that she was, turned away from his marred features even while he writhed in the pain of transformation.

The following day, she had her grandfather petition to break the engagement on the grounds of his 'ruined beauty.' Vitalia could have denied the petition, and even sued Karjala for not honoring the contract, but Sebastian didn't have the will to fight. He had no desire to force a woman into an unwanted marriage and after her behavior, he wasn't sure he even wanted to see Lacey again, never mind marry her.

"Lacey behaved abominably," Sebastian said evenly, breaking his reverie. "But she has ruined enough of my life; she doesn't get to taint anymore of it. I have to believe that not all women are as shallow and faithless as her."

"Good for you. And maybe if you find a wife, Philippe will give me some breathing space. He and Marianne keep inviting eligible nobles to visit and he is pushing me to accept one. But they are all such bores."

"Do you need me to come up to the Palace? I can use my brotherly veto to get rid of the bores for you."

"How many vetoes do you have? It seems like Marianne finds a dozen men a day to come court me. I don't know how she convinces so many to show up."

Sebastian almost snorted but caught himself just in

time. Only a day, and he had already picked up that undignified habit from Sienna! But really, Eva didn't seem to understand her own charms. It was not an accident that their mother called her the Fairest. As a child, she had always been pretty, but as she matured she blossomed into true beauty. Nearly ten years her senior, it was hard for Sebastian to be objective about his sister's charms, but there was never a shortage of men vying for her attention. Even Marcus remarked on her beauty when he accompanied Sebastian to her sixteenth birthday party. The only reason Sebastian hadn't punched his best friend for it was that he knew Marcus considered himself Eva's third older brother, and so the comment was harmless.

"So what made you think of marriage again?"

"Well, having the new Ranger trainee in the castle reminded me of what it could be like to have a lady here all the time and I realized I missed it."

"Wait, you accepted a *woman* as a Ranger trainee? And she's staying in the castle instead of the barracks? What did Marcus say? Did he flip a lid?"

"Mrs. Chambers insisted that a woman couldn't sleep in the Barracks with the soldiers, so she's been put in the blue suite instead. And Marcus was skeptical about admitting a woman until she beat him in combat by poisoning his weapon."

"Marcus was poisoned?" Eva shrieked. "Is he hurt? Did you call a medic?"

"Calm down, sis. He's fine. Sienna had the antidote with her and gave it to him immediately. She just did it to prove a point, which she made rather effectively."

"Sienna?"

"Yes, why?"

"I knew a Sienna once..."

"Well, Sienna is her nickname. Her proper name is

Carissa Antonella and she's Cadizan. She hasn't said much about her background, but I would judge her to be upper-level Bourgeoisie, based on how well-spoken she is. Maybe even low-ranking aristocracy."

"Not the same person then," Eva concluded. "Though I would like to meet her someday. Anyone who can surprise and best both you and Marcus definitely deserves notice!"

"Right, that's enough of that, I think. Don't you have a soirée of suitors to attend?"

"Yes, and I've already missed half of it, but Marianne won't scold me when I tell her I was talking to you. You can do no wrong after all, golden boy."

"And I suppose in your version, I called you and refused to let you go even though you told me about the soirée at the very start?" Sebastian asked, amused.

"Of course!" Eva grinned mischievously. "Goodnight brother, dearest."

"Goodnight Eva. My love to Philippe and Marianne. Try to enjoy the soirée."

"Oh, and Sebastian," she called, just as she was swiping the mirror clear. "Lose the hood!" The mirror snapped back to normal; Eva had broken the connection and left Sebastian staring at his own reflection. For a moment, he was transfixed by the shadowy features hidden in the recesses of his hood. His hand hovered at the edge of the hood as he debated whether to pull it back. He slammed the mirror back onto his desk face down.

"Not tonight Eva," he whispered apologetically. And though he didn't say it, he couldn't help thinking the addendum that throbbed in his mind.

Maybe not ever.

4

She thought it was her imagination at first but as the session went on she became certain of it; Sebastian was ignoring her. Oh, he had been perfectly polite to her, friendly even, both at breakfast and when he arrived at the training room, but since the training started it was like she was invisible to him. He focused on the others in the room, Rangers and recruits alike, adjusting their technique, giving advice or the rare praise, but it seemed the lone female in the room was not worth his attention. She got plenty of attention from the other men though. They all watched her, some curious, some hostile, some leering, but she didn't care about them. She had come here to be trained by the best, and she refused to allow Sebastian of Vitalia to disregard her after she had passed his test and gained his promise of instruction.

The session ended and the rest of the class congregated together chatting among themselves. She could still feel their eyes on her and she wasn't sure how she would handle walking into the mess hall with them and the rest of the Rangers for lunch. She had kept her head down after class as she gathered her things in a vain attempt to not draw attention, but she felt the shadow fall across her. *So, it begins,* she thought apprehensively. But when she looked up it was to see Sir Marcus smiling at her.

"We're going back to the castle for lunch. Are you coming with us?" Beyond him, she could see Sebastian waiting, so she could guess who 'we' comprised. She wished she could see his expression to gauge what he thought of Marcus' invitation, but as usual, it was hidden by his hood. His posture though was open and welcoming rather than reluctant, so considering the alternative she decided that joining them sounded like a good option. She tried to ignore the mutterings from the other recruits as she left the training room with the Captain and the Prince. From the slight frown that appeared on Marcus' face, she guessed that he had heard also and wasn't happy about it. He engaged her in light conversation on their walk to the castle, putting her at ease. Sebastian was silent throughout. Of the two of them, Sienna found it strange that it was Marcus who had forgiven her for the silver nutmeg first. In fact, he seemed to admire her for it. Sebastian just seemed irked that he was forced to let her stay and train because of it.

Rather than go to the dining hall as Sienna expected, Sebastian led them to a small parlor room, clearly designed for more intimate dining and interactions. The tea was on the table waiting for them when they arrived, and Sienna was surprised to see three places set. They had clearly expected that she would dine with them, rather than it being a last-minute addition as she had surmised. Mrs. Chambers was still laying out the luncheon in a buffet spread on a side table as the three of them sat down. Sebastian poured the tea as he told them his decision.

"I have decided it's time to end my seclusion, so I am going to attend the Harbor Ball next week."

Marcus almost choked on his tea. "You have got to be kidding me!" he laughed.

Sienna could see from the stiffness of Sebastian's shoulders that he was not kidding and that he was affronted by his friend's reaction.

"What's the Harbor Ball?" Sienna asked, drawing both men's attention to herself thus diffusing the tension building between them.

"It's the premier social event this side of the summer solstice," Marcus explained animatedly. "It marks the end of the rough seas of winter when the trading ships can start to dock in Vitalia again. The noble and merchant classes all come together to celebrate the start of the new trading season, and the influx of new products and information it brings. Everyone who's anyone in Port Royale attends, with one noticeable exception. I can't remember the last time Sebastian went to any social function he wasn't forced to by his family!"

"Well, I'm going this year," Sebastian said. "You should come too, and join our party," he added, turning to Sienna. She looked at him in stunned surprise for a moment then burst out laughing.

"It's a good thing everyone knows you're a genius, Sebastian, or they would think you an idiot for saying things like that!" she chortled. Looking at his stiff posture, she realized that he had made the invitation in earnest and couldn't see what was wrong with it. "You can't expect to meet ladies you would be interested in courting if you arrive with another woman in tow," she explained.

"Lunch is served," Mrs. Chambers said, startling them all. She curtseyed to Sebastian as she left the room but Sienna caught a disdainful glare directed her way before the housekeeper closed the door behind her.

"She's right, you know," Marcus said, continuing their

conversation as he helped himself to the cold meats laid out on the sideboard. For the sake of Sebastian's feelings, Marcus contained his merriment at his friend's faux-pas and Sienna's teasing, but his green eyes still sparkled with amusement. "But you should still come, Sienna. A large group of Rangers goes each year, depending on who's in residence at the time, so you can attend without having to accompany His Obliviousness."

"Maybe I will go," Sienna agreed, a plan beginning to form in her mind. She needed to show Sebastian that she was more than just a smaller, weaker man, that she had other, *different*, skills and attributes that could be valuable to him. Maybe this was her opportunity to prove herself to him. She knew he was having some difficulty with the Hamm brothers, and from the sounds of the Harbor Ball, there was no way the leading merchant family in the city would miss it. She could use the event to gain a better understanding of the issues and maybe even find a solution!

"Talk to Mrs. Chambers about a dress," Sebastian instructed. "She will be able to get a seamstress to come here to take your measurements and get something to your liking ready in time. Your stipend as a Ranger recruit should more than cover what you need."

Sienna appreciated the consideration from the Prince, so when lunch was finished she went in search of the housekeeper to discuss a dress for the ball. She found her in her office and waited for the curt 'come in' in response to her knock before entering.

"Sebastian said I should talk to you about getting a dress made for the Harbor Ball?"

"I thought you weren't going to attend the Ball?" Mrs. Chambers queried archly. Sienna was surprised by the veiled hostility but plowed on. She needed the support of the Housekeeper and the rest of the staff if she was to pull this off.

"I won't be attending with the Prince and his party, but I do intend to go separately."

"Then you'll need a gown. Have you any thoughts on what you want?"

"Yes, something in Orellan fabric but Bretonnian in style, low neck, tight bodice, lots of ruffles."

"A tart's dress," Mrs. Chambers sneered.

"Exactly!" Sienna smiled, pleased that the other woman understood her vision. But then her mood soured as she realized that she had not told Mrs. Chambers her intention to disguise herself to infiltrate the party, so she thought that this dress was Sienna's own style. The full rudeness of the remark struck Sienna, and she realized she had a choice to make. She could feign obliviousness and accept the Housekeeper's disdain for who she thought Sienna was in return for her assistance. Or she could challenge her attitude and either gain a true ally or lose any hope of support, depending on how she reacted to being called out. Sienna bit her lip but really, there was no choice. If she was going to suffer the cool distance the Housekeeper had put between them she wanted to at least know why, and have the right of reply.

"Mrs. Chambers, may I be bluntly honest with you?" Sienna asked, steeling herself. "I get the impression that you don't think much of me, and I would like to know why."

Mrs. Chambers stared at her coolly for so long that Sienna thought she wouldn't answer. "You're not very respectful of the Master," she sniffed finally. Inwardly, Sienna sighed with relief. At least this was a charge she could defend herself on.

"On the contrary," Sienna said. "I have the utmost respect for him. I wouldn't be here if I didn't think his skills are the greatest in all Fable. I think what you mean is that I am not very *deferential* to him. But I don't see why I should be. As a swordsman, a military leader, and a strategist I fully acknowledge his superiority to me, but as a man? No, I don't believe some people are 'better' than others, just because an accident of birth gave them a title, or wealth, or both."

"Hmph, you're one of *those* sorts then. Anti-establishment, and all that."

"Absolutely not. I believe the monarchy plays a vital role in all kingdoms as arbiters of the peace and dispensers of justice, which is the backbone of society. But that breaks down the moment some members of society think they are 'better' than others or 'entitled' because of the family they come from rather than for their own achievements or hard work.

"Take Sebastian for example." Mrs. Chambers winced. She probably thought Sienna's casual use of the master's given name was impertinent but Sienna ignored it, on a roll. "He is a prince, first in line for the throne. He could have sat back idly, lived a life of debauchery and excess, and there would be no consequences because the nobility would still revere him. But he wasn't satisfied to presume on the good fortune he had been granted and trained in the army so he would have practical skills of his own. His title meant he could have started his career as a senior officer, but he chose to work up the ranks instead, earning him the unwavering loyalty of the most deadly force on the continent. It also is what gave him the understanding of how the army's different factions work that enabled him to propose the daring strategy that changed the course of the Battle of El Salia, in opposition to the wishes of the generals who would have sent those soldiers to be slaughtered. *That* is what makes him a great man, *that's* why I respect and admire him; being a prince is irrelevant."

“It’s not many who would disregard being royalty so easily.”

Sienna shrugged. “It’s how I was raised. My father always said that a person’s value should be measured by their personal accomplishments, not by what was handed to them. Unfortunately, he thought that my accomplishments should be limited to music, drawing, and dancing; learning to fight, to protect myself, was not an acceptable aspiration.”

Mrs. Chambers looked hard at her, assessing her words. Sienna waited silently for the verdict. Finally, the housekeeper nodded.

“Perhaps I misjudged you,” she conceded. “You’ll do fine here.”

5

"His Majesty King Philippe to see you, sir," the butler announced.

"Send him in Butler," Sebastian replied. It wasn't like he was unaware that his brother was coming, the furor from the courtyard and stables for the last fifteen minutes was enough of a clue. Philippe bustled in, as full of motion and energy as Sebastian was self-contained. Their temperaments were so different it was sometimes hard to tell they were brothers, never mind twins. Of course, you only had to look at them to know the relationship, given they were identical. Or at least, they used to be, before the curse changed everything.

"Send up tea and some of those delicious little pastries that Chef makes, would you Butler? And make sure my men have something to eat too before we have to go back?"

"Of course, sire," Butler replied, bowing as he left the room. Moments later the tea trolley was wheeled in and left discretely beside them to help themselves. Sebastian waited patiently for Philippe to finally settle himself and get to the point of his visit. It must be something important if he felt the need to come to Port Royale in person rather than just call on the magic mirror.

"So Eva tells me you've finally decided to find a wife again," Philippe started. *That would do it*, Sebastian thought to himself, but remained silent. "I came straight away to discuss the possible candidates with you."

Sebastian frowned. "There's nothing to discuss yet. I'm attending the Harbor Ball next week. I'll let you know after that if there is anyone who has caught my attention."

"The Harbor Ball?" Philippe spluttered aghast. "That's fine if you want a dalliance – and by all means, feel free – but it is no place to find a *wife*. Are you thinking of marrying a merchant girl? Gad, the thought!"

"I am thinking of marrying someone I love."

"Don't be naïve. You're not a boy anymore. You're a prince, you have to marry the right sort. I've been building a list ever since that unfortunate incident with Princess Lacey. I have the details with me."

Sebastian snorted. His family never knew how to talk about those events, but 'unfortunate incident' was the most banal euphemism he had heard for it so far. It somehow fell short of capturing the full impact of the betrayal by his faithless fiancée at the lowest point in his life. He let it go. Making his brother uncomfortable by confronting him about it was not his objective today. Instead, he resigned himself to the other part of the conversation, knowing Philippe would not accept a refusal until he had made his case in full. "So, who do you have on this list then?"

Philippe shuffled his papers, glad Sebastian was being reasonable about this. He pulled up his first candidate. "Princess Aurora of Northaven."

"The 'Desperate Debutante?' She must have courted every prince, duke, and squire since she came out three years ago!"

"But she hasn't accepted any of them, and she *is* a princess."

"She's also sixteen! I want a woman, not a simpering child. Next."

"Lady Tremaine."

"The Baron of Burtz's widow? From one extreme to the other, Philippe. She's old enough to be our mother!"

"You're exaggerating. She still has childbearing years ahead of her and has already proven her fertility."

"So the two obnoxious brats are part of the package? No. Just, no."

"Um, well, what about the Orellan princess?" Philippe suggested desperately.

"You know I've always liked Violetta. But unless I am seriously misinformed – and *that* is unlikely – she is still married to the son of the Duke of Behr and expecting their second child in a few months."

"Not her, you dolt. Her sister, Princess Olivia."

"Olivia doesn't like men, Philippe. I want a wife that at least has a chance of loving me."

"What about the other sister?"

"She's as young as Aurora!" Sebastian burst out in exasperation. "Seriously Philippe, your list is terrible! I'm going to attend the Harbor Ball and let nature take its course. You married for love; why shouldn't I?"

"Because you're my heir! You're six minutes younger than me and you're the only heir I have!" Sebastian sat back, shocked. He had never seen his brother so agitated.

"I love Marianne, but we've tried and tried and still we have no children. We could deflect the expectations for a while, but we're running out of time. There are mutterings in the court and even some of my advisors have started to hint that if the queen can't give me an heir that I should put her aside and find a new wife who can. I say that you are my heir, but you have no children either so where does the crown pass to? Do we hand over the kingdom to whoever Eva marries? You know the sharks are circling her already on that expectation. Marianne is more than just my queen, my wife. She is my everything. I love her, but if we don't have children and you don't have children to inherit the throne, they are going to try to annul our marriage. I can't lose her, Sebastian, I can't! I would abdicate before I would give her up!"

"Blast it, Philippe, why didn't you come to me sooner? Of course, we won't let them take Marianne from you. She's family."

PHILIPPE LET out a breath he hadn't realized he was holding. "I didn't want to burden you with this or pressure you into a relationship before you were ready. I –" He was interrupted by the door opening, and he was further surprised when a very pretty young woman entered without knocking or waiting for acknowledgment from within. She looked at him briefly as she scanned the room.

"I'm sorry Sebastian, I didn't realize you had company." *A very pretty young woman who is on a first-name basis with my brother*, Philippe amended.

"That's no problem. Is there something you need?"

"I just wanted to borrow your copy of *Of Weapons and Warfare*. Marcus is being stubborn about the effective use of maces in a skirmish, and I can't find a copy in the library."

Sebastian pulled the book from his shelves and handed it to her. "Here you go." He was smiling, Philippe could hear it in his voice. Who was this woman?

"Thanks, sorry for interrupting. See you at dinner?" He nodded and she smiled at him, then turned in Philippe's direction and dropped a curtsey. "Your Majesty." Philippe narrowed his eyes at her as she closed the door behind her. So she *had* known who he was and still dismissed him. Ignorance was one thing; insolence something else entirely. "Who was that?" he demanded.

"That's Carissa Antonella, the newest Ranger recruit."

"You let a woman into the Rangers?" Philippe asked, shocked. He frowned as he replayed the conversation he had just witnessed. "You are having dinner together and are intimate enough that she calls you by your given name; is she your mistress?"

Sebastian choked on his tea. "*Zut alors*, no! She joins me for mealtimes because Mrs. Chambers insisted that she couldn't sleep in the barracks with the other recruits and had to stay in the castle instead, and you know that all my Rangers call me by my name and not my title. It's good for morale."

"If you say so," Philippe was still dubious. Girls who looked like *that* did not aspire to be soldiers or spies. "But please make sure she stays out of sight when you bring a lady you are courting to visit you here. You don't want a misunderstanding to derail a marriage prospect."

"Don't worry, Philippe, I won't let that happen. And I won't let anyone forcibly annul your marriage either. There is no precedent in Vitalian law that would allow them to do so; the decision is yours alone, so you and Marianne can put your hearts at rest. You will make great parents in time, and my marriage will buy you that time. It will work out, you'll see."

"Thank you, Sebastian." Philippe sat back in his chair, the heavy weight of worry lifted from his mind. He snagged another of the small flaky pastries he loved so much and ate his fill while they spoke of other things.

~

OVER AN HOUR LATER, the brothers walked back to the grand hallway, where the King's retinue had assembled waiting for their master's signal to leave. Sebastian took a moment to greet the Ranger who was the King's primary guard, then stood back as the usual flurry of activity enveloped Philippe before he was gone. Once the courtyard was clear, Sebastian made his way back to his study. He loved his brother, but his visits were exhausting, even when they weren't so emotionally fraught. He picked up the papers Philippe had left describing all his recommendations. He hesitated a moment, then shoved them into a drawer.

"I will find a wife soon, Philippe," he promised. "But I'll find her my own way."

6

"There. What do you think?"

Sienna looked at herself in the full-length mirror as Mrs. Chambers continued to fuss around her. As requested, the dress was covered in layers of ruffles in a garish red trimmed with gold.

"It's perfect!"

"Are you sure it's not too much?" Mrs. Chambers fretted. "I know you said you want a tart's dress but..."

"If you want to catch anything you have to use the right bait. And tonight I need to catch the attention of the bourgeoisie – particularly the young ladies of that set. This ensemble is just gaudy enough to attract their attention, without making me seem like a threat. They are looking for husbands after all; I'm just looking for information."

"Do you think you'll be able to get what you need? The Master hasn't said anything of course, but a good servant knows when trouble is brewing. We can all see something is bothering him so anything you can do to help makes you golden in our eyes."

"Thank you, Mrs. Chambers, I couldn't do this without you."

"You're welcome, my dear. Now, come with me. If you want to get to your transport without the Master or his party seeing you, you can leave via the kitchens. And you can return that way also – I'll be waiting to hear how it goes."

Sienna took one last look in the mirror. She pulled the neckline of her dress down further to make her modest cleavage appear more prominent and added jewelry made from the finest Orellan glass to draw the eye and complete the charade. *If you want to make a sale, you have to display your wares*, she muttered to herself. One final check in the mirror and she gave her reflection a satisfied nod before following Mrs. Chambers to the servants' entrance.

Butler was waiting by the door.

"Miss Sienna, you look..." He trailed off, words failing him?

"Garish? Tacky?" Sienna suggested laughingly.

"*Appropriate*," he settled on.

"I'll take it!" Her laughter drifted back on the breeze as she hurried outside. At the stables, the second coachman already had a small chaise and four rigged up for her. He took her hand and helped her into her seat.

"I'll be your driver tonight, Miss Antonella," he told her. "And may I say I wouldn't have known it was you if I didn't know, if you know what I mean?"

"Indeed I do, Olivier, and thank you. That is the idea, after all."

He gave her a shy smile then climbed into his own seat. With a flick of the reins they were off, and Sienna pondered what she might learn at the Harbor Ball.

~

"WELL, THAT WAS A DISASTER," Sebastian huffed in disgust. How had it gone so wrong? He had been charming and complimentary all evening, even to the vacuous gigglers. Well, he may have rolled his eyes when one asked if he found it dull to have to read so many books, but it was not like she could have seen the gesture with his hood up. He tried to ignore the whispers about why he wore the hood that were flying around the room, but no one was being particularly subtle. Even those passing along the story of his cursed face seemed shocked at his shrouded appearance. Things started to improve when he asked Lady Alicia to dance. They continued talking after they left the floor and Lady Alicia proposed they take a walk in the gardens. He couldn't understand why she got so upset at his suggestion she should fetch her cloak to cover up before going outside. It was still chilly at night and she had a lot of skin exposed; she would have been freezing! She glared at him indignantly, then made that snide remark about *his* cloak, saying not everyone needed to hide themselves under lots of material. Then she flounced off, leaving him alone and perplexed on the terrace. He was being chivalrous and she acted as if he had suggested something lewd!

Maybe Philippe was right, maybe his circumstances weren't suitable to meeting a potential bride naturally. At least if it were an arranged match, she would know what to expect and wouldn't be upset by his appearance. Resigned, he opened the drawer he had so glibly stuck the list in and started perusing the contents. He skipped over the ones Philippe had already pitched and started reading.

Once he got over his fundamental objection to the concept of an arranged marriage, he realized that the ladies shortlisted by Philippe weren't terrible. He marked a couple as he read through for a deeper examination later. A little over halfway through he stopped. Lady Camilla, the Duke of Belgravia's daughter, was twenty-two, listed reading and politics as her interests and drawing, horse riding, and playing the harpsichord among her accomplishments. And she was Vitalian. If he wasn't marrying a princess, choosing a Vitalian aristocrat rather than a foreign one would be popular with the people and might soothe the court's ire over Marianne's origins. He looked at the portrait included with the personal summary. He wondered if she had drawn it herself. Large brown eyes twinkled at him above full lips drawn back in a secret smile. Waves of golden hair framed her face. She was undoubtedly beautiful and he was surprised that she wasn't married already. But then he considered that she was of an age with Eva. He supposed the best ladies could afford to wait to ensure they found the best match, rather than accepting the first man who proposed to them. And the extra maturity would be helpful in navigating this path together. He didn't need some starry-eyed teenager dreaming of true love's kiss and happily ever after. Hopefully, that would come in time, of course, but you couldn't expect it from the first meeting. Perhaps Lady Camilla was the partner he could work with to achieve that end while still acknowledging the pragmatic realities of a royal marriage until then. She certainly seemed like the perfect fit for him, eclipsing all the other potential candidates.

Sebastian sighed. It was time to admit that Philippe had been right. He picked up his magic mirror.

"Mirror, mirror, in my hand, Show me the strongest in the land."

The mirror's surface rippled and a moment later Philippe's face appeared in the frame. Sebastian always found it disconcerting to look at the reflection that should have been his, but was no more.

"I looked at your list of candidates," Sebastian said without preamble. Philippe's attention sharpened instantly.

"I would like to arrange a meeting with Lady Camilla of Belgravia." Philippe broke into a huge grin.

"I knew you would like Camilla! She was my first choice for you."

"If you thought she was so suitable, why didn't you lead with her when we spoke a week ago?" Sebastian asked, exasperated.

"Because I know you! If I had led with Lady Camilla you would have rejected her on principle without learning anything about her and then I would never have gotten you to consider her." Sebastian thought of Princess Aurora, Lady Tremaine, and the Orellan sisters he had disregarded without a second glance and ruefully conceded that Philippe had a point. His brother knew him too well.

"If you want to get to know her, the best thing to do is host her there in Port Royale for a few weeks. You can arrange some dinners and balls for her, and interact with her in both formal and informal settings. We can work out the actual details of the marriage pact afterward, as long as you two can reach an agreement in principle to marry by the end of the visit."

"Sure," Sebastian agreed weakly. He was meant to be the bravest, but suddenly he was feeling overwhelmed. "How soon do you think you can arrange for her to come?"

"I'll send the invitation at once. I'll suggest an arrival date a month from today, for a fortnight's visit. That should give you enough time to prepare, and enough time to propose. I'm sure she will agree to the timings – I hinted at the possibility to her before and she seemed very keen." Sebastian only shook his head; Philippe really did know him too well to predict his capitulation and choice. They said their goodbyes and Sebastian set the mirror down. The die was cast now and based on all he knew, he felt confident of a favorable outcome. He needed to get ready though, and the first step was to tell Butler and Mrs. Chambers.

His future bride was coming to visit.

Mrs. Chambers took the news with a disapproving frown at the lack of notice. Butler was stoic. Both were determined to ensure the household and additional entertainments ran perfectly for the visit; they wouldn't allow anything to mar this opportunity for their beloved master. As a result, every servant in the castle was in a frenzy for the next month to prepare the perfect welcome to Port Royale for their future mistress.

Marcus was surprised by his decision, but wholeheartedly supportive. Sienna's reaction took *him* by surprise. He hadn't really expected any reaction from her, he supposed, so her overwhelming enthusiasm and congratulations blindsided him. She was as excited about the prospect of a wedding as, well, as a seventeen-year-old girl, Sebastian concluded ruefully. But he was further surprised when he realized that her excitement was not the general female obsession with weddings and parties; she was excited on *his* behalf. Her unshakeable belief that he deserved to be happy reminded him of his sister. *It is nice having someone so completely in your corner*, he admitted to himself, even if he refused to acknowledge it out loud.

He noticed that she missed a few training sessions in the week that followed his announcement, and was distracted at mealtimes. Though he still thought it was a waste of his time training her when it was clear she couldn't keep up with the other recruits, he worried that perhaps his neglect had pushed her away. Was she going to quit the Red Hoods after all? Contrarily, the thought irritated him. He didn't want her to join in the first place and still didn't think she belonged, but he had just started getting used to having her around. It would be most inconsiderate of her to leave now and make him have to readjust to his solitary pursuits again.

He was pondering this one evening, sitting at the dining table alone and staring at Sienna's empty seat. Was this the day she was going to announce she was leaving? Or was she already gone? Come to think of it, he hadn't seen her all day. But surely she would not have left without saying good-bye...? He heard her voice in the corridor calling something to Mrs. Chambers. *So, she's still here*, he thought, and felt somewhat relieved to note she sounded upbeat and cheery and not like she was about to admit defeat and quit. He admired her resilience, if nothing else.

Sienna almost danced into the dining room, seemingly unconcerned that she was late for the start of the meal. "I think I have a solution to your problems with the Hamm Brothers!" she said breezily taking her seat beside him and reaching to help herself to the dishes arrayed.

Sebastian was taken aback. He thought she was about to quit and instead it seemed that she had been out meddling in things she couldn't understand. He had mentioned the Hamm Brothers once in passing to her; what could she know of his dealings with them? He nodded to the servants to indicate they should leave. When he was sure there was no one left to overhear, he turned to look at her. "What problems exactly do you presume I have?" he asked imperiously.

"Well, they are defying your orders about the quality of their building materials at every opportunity. If it was just Stupid Hamm or Smarmy Hamm, you could dismiss it as ignorance, but you know Shrewd Hamm is calling the shots here. He seems to be angling for a showdown between the nobility and the merchant classes. If you push the point too hard and insist they remove the sub-standard constructions, he will accuse you of abusing royal power to oppress the people who are working hard to make Vitalia prosperous and great. But if you do nothing, he will claim that royalty is powerless in the face of the people's wishes and push for further concessions and favors that will be in no one's interest other than the Hamms'. How am I doing so far?"

Sebastian had to admit, if only to himself, that she was right on the money and he wondered how she got her information. The Hamms were stirring up a lot of discontent among the merchant classes, and the possibility of those anti-monarchy sentiments gaining traction had been a source of concern for him and Philippe for some time. Aloud, all he said was "Go on."

"Shrewd Hamm is irked that though he is wealthier than half the nobles in the city, they still look down on him because he is 'just a laborer.' His aspiration is to be knighted or otherwise welcomed into the fold, and he has cultivated a friendship with Lady Penelope de Chezon to this end. She invites him and his brothers to her soirées and introduces them to her friends. Shrewd wins over the gentlemen, while Smarmy charms the ladies. And behind the scenes, certain luxuries now beyond Lady Penelope's means despite the pedigree of her family name, will appear at Chezon Hall courtesy of the Hamm coffers." All of this tallied with what Sebastian already knew. One of his agents had long since infiltrated the de Chezon soirées to keep watch over Shrewd Hamm and his friends but had not found evidence of unfair dealings. Instead, his spy reported that a worrying number of the aristocracy would follow Lady Penelope's lead in supporting the Hamms. Though he was impressed with how quickly Sienna had gathered her own intelligence, he was disappointed that she had nothing new to offer him. He settled into his seat to listen to the rest of her story.

"Now, Lady Penelope has a niece, an impressionable girl only just coming out. Cécile has been caught in the sway of Smarmy Hamm, and has already been, shall we say, 'indiscrete' with him." Sebastian leaned forward. A scandal? "Oh, nothing reputation-destroying, at least not yet," Sienna reassured him. "But enough to generate those snide remarks that the aristocracy seems to thrive on, were it more widely known. But the real threat to Lady Penelope's continued patronage is not that Smarmy is courting her niece but that she is not the only one he is courting!" That *did* surprise Sebastian. He knew about Smarmy and Cécile, but not about any other women. He was glad his hood hid his expressions, so he could retain his aura of omniscience. Sienna grinned at him before continuing.

"Marie Jobert, the Vintner's daughter, has been entertaining her friends in the Bourgeoisie with tales of her liaison with Smarmy and his commentary on the insipid and vacuous noble – not his words, obviously, I'm paraphrasing – he is forced to make nice with. His exact words were, I believe, 'It's lucky she's a de Chezon because it is the only thing in her favor. But really, how much is that name even worth these days?' I can't imagine Lady P would be pleased to hear such things. Shrewd Hamm understands business, but for all his aspirations he doesn't understand the aristocracy. He thinks that Lady P will bow to his will because of his money; he doesn't understand that though she is poor she is proud, and that family pride is the foundation of the noble classes. She would rather suffer poverty than the indignity of her family honor being slighted in such a way."

Sebastian was slightly dazed by the volume of information she had just thrown at him. She was right about Lady Penelope's reaction should she learn that one of the Hamm brothers had been belittling her family – and it made him wonder how Sienna understood the mind-set of the aristocracy so well. However, hearsay and rumors were too easy to deny. He needed to be surer before he could attempt to separate Hamm from the social sponsorship of the de Chezon family.

"How did you come to learn what Mademoiselle Jobert is discussing with her close friends?"

"Signor di Constanza, one of the premier Orellan Glassworkers, arrived in port a week ago. He was accompanied on the voyage by his daughter Lucia. Lucia attended the Harbor Ball that evening and was an instant sensation with the other ladies from the Bourgeoisie families, due to the exquisite glass jewelry she was displaying and the gossip of new music and dances from Orella and her trading partners in the Orient. She was introduced to Marie that night, and then met her the following afternoon while strolling down Rue des Nantis. Realizing that Lucia's father's business was keeping him from accompanying her, Marie took Lucia under her wing and the two have been bosom friends for the past four days."

"And?" Sebastian prompted impatiently, not sure where she was going with this tangent.

"Oh," said Sienna, seeming surprised that he wasn't following her. "Don't you see? *I'm* Lucia."

"You were at the Harbor Ball? I didn't see you."

"*I* wasn't there, *Lucia* was. Big hair, garish dress, obnoxiously loud laugh?"

Sebastian thought back to the disastrous night that had been the ball. There was only one person the description fit – a showy, tacky, woman who talked too loudly and whose laugh had grated on his ears. He had been relieved that she had been engrossed with her own set and had shown no interest in trying to snare the prince. "That was *you*?"

"Mostly, people see what they expect to see, and overlook what they don't. You didn't expect me to be at the Ball when I didn't travel with the Rangers, nor that a vulgar debutante was your Ranger trainee. Context is a better disguise than any costume."

Sebastian sat back stunned. His spies had been working for *months* trying – and failing – to find some leverage he could use against the Hamm family, and Sienna had achieved it in less than a week. Furthermore, while he had just been wondering about her possible links with the aristocracy herself, this charade demonstrated a deep and nuanced understanding of the merchants to accurately determine the right bait to attract and lure them in. Being able to switch between classes and blend in both was an admirable and important skillset for an intelligence officer, but it left him no closer to knowing Sienna's true origins.

The mystery of Sienna's origins would have to wait. Right now, he needed to address the tantalizing lead she had found. "Do you believe her, the Jobert girl?"

"Yes, absolutely. She is neither creative enough nor vindictive enough to have made the story up."

"But do you have any proof, other than her word?"

"Hamm gave her his signet ring. She wears it on a chain around her neck, but she showed it to me."

"Could it have been a gift before he met Lady Penelope's niece? A remnant of a now-broken courtship?" Sebastian fired the questions at her, making sure their case was watertight. He could not afford the misstep of an unverified accusation.

"I saw him wearing the same ring the day I visited his grandfather's workshop to get the key to your study. And Mademoiselle Cécile had arrived at her aunt's by then. And he wasn't wearing the ring when I saw him more recently, so it isn't a copy that Marie has that could affect the timing. No,

Carlos 'Smarmy' Hamm gave his ring to Marie Jobert, and he did so after he started courting Cécile de Chezon."

"We have him," Sebastian smiled in wonder.

"We have him," Sienna confirmed with satisfaction.

"I'll have the Magistrate arrange a meeting with Diego Hamm for tomorrow to inform him that his timber constructions will no longer be tolerated and that he no longer has the support he would need to defy us. I will call on Lady Penelope myself in advance to appraise her of the situation and ensure her support is withdrawn. I can't believe the stand-off is finally coming to an end!"

Sebastian was mentally kicking himself. All this time he had been disregarding Sienna because she didn't fit his predefined mold of what a Red Hood should be. But she had proven that different didn't mean defective. He had to stop criticizing her for not being a man and find ways to capitalize on her advantages as a woman. And he had to acknowledge that she deserved her place among the Rangers as much if not more than every other recruit in the barracks. He raised his glass toward her.

"A toast," he said. "To Carissa Antonella, who may be the littlest of the Red Hoods but is by no means the least."

Sienna smiled as she clinked glasses with him.

7

Diego Hamm strode out of the Magistrate's office the next day, fuming. He was known as 'Shrewd' for his cunning and business acumen, yet he had been well and truly checkmated. What he couldn't work out is how the Prince had heard about Marie and Carlos. It's not like they moved in the same circles. Deep in his own thoughts, he tuned out his playboy brother greeting every female on the street until something nagged at his attention. He looked up to see a pretty girl hurrying past with only a murmured "Monsieur Hamm" in acknowledgment.

"Who is that girl, Carlos?" he asked.

"She's one of Marie's friends, Lucia di Constanza. She came on the ships from Orella and they struck up a friendship at the Harbor Ball."

Diego turned to watch her and saw her heading toward the office they had just left. It all clicked into place. It was *nervousness* he had heard in her voice and seen on her face. This unknown girl, who was friends with Marie and was now casually chatting with two Rangers.

"So that's how he knew," Diego murmured, still watching her. "Well played, sir."

"Who knew what?" Carlos asked, staring at his brother.

"The Prince. That friend of Marie's is his informant."

Carlos whipped round to see Lucia again. She was standing there, blithely waving goodbye to a couple of Red Hoods as if they were old friends. He marched toward her, fury in every step. Diego realized too late that he had lit the fuse and hurried after his brother. By the time he caught up, Carlos had already seized the girl by the arm and slammed her up against the wall of an alleyway.

"What did you do, you stupid cow?" he snarled at her.

SIENNA'S HEAD bounced against the wall from the force she was shoved with. The combined impact of pain and surprise froze her in place, while her mind filled with panic. Carlos Hamm was no longer the charming rogue; he didn't even look smarmy anymore. Right now, Carlos Hamm looked *scary*. His face was suffused with rage, and there was a malevolent gleam in his eyes that promised extreme unpleasantness. Sienna had seen a similar look before on another man's face; she knew how bad it could become.

The face of her kidnapper superimposed itself over the man in front of her, as memory swallowed her. Piper, the only name she knew him by, lunged at her furiously. She was the only one left, and he would make her pay. Fear paralyzed her limbs. "Please, Monsieur, let me go," she pleaded. Was that her voice, sounding so weak and scared? She felt sick to her stomach.

"And why would I let a pretty thing like you go?" Smarmy asked. His voice pulled her back to the present, though it was not much of an improvement over her flashback. Terror still gnawed at her insides. Smarmy leered at her. There was nothing sexual about that leer, it was a look designed to intimidate. Sienna hated to admit it, but it was rather effective in that goal. She looked to the mouth of the alleyway, where Shrewd Hamm stood, hoping he would intervene. The expression on his face did nothing to reassure her. He wasn't certain he could rein his brother in, and more frightening, she saw a hint that he wasn't sure if he wanted to. He stalked toward Sienna, still pinned to the wall by Carlos' strong arms.

"How do you know Prince Sebastian, Mademoiselle di Constanza?" he demanded, his voice all the more menacing for remaining in a conversational tone.

"What?"

"Don't play coy," he snapped. "Somehow the Prince found out about Carlos and Marie, despite the fact they have been very discrete. And now we find you outside the Magistrate's office palling around with the Prince's Rangers. So start talking, Lucia."

Lucia. The name echoed in Sienna's addled mind. *They still think I'm Lucia. They don't know...*

"I don't know anything about the Prince," she stammered, hoping that the lie would lessen their fury. She turned to address Smarmy directly. "I went to the Magistrate to tell him to make that aristocrat leave you alone. Marie deserves a man she doesn't have to share."

"Did Marie ask you to intercede on her behalf?" Shrewd asked in a low voice.

"No."

"Then why do you think you have the right to interfere in our business, *putain*?" Smarmy yelled at her. He pulled his arm back to hit her. Sienna cowered in fear, waiting for the punch to land but instead, a shout from the main street made her look up. A Ranger stood there, taking in the scene. Smarmy straightened up and Sienna quickly slipped past him to the Ranger's side.

"What's going on here?" the Ranger asked, looking between them.

"Everything is fine," Shrewd said smoothly. "My brother just got a little over-amorous; you know his reputation. But can you blame him with such a pretty girl?" Shrewd ran a finger down Sienna's cheek. She wanted to recoil from his touch but the look in his eyes warned her not to. She shivered involuntarily. She would take the unconcealed rage in Smarmy's eyes over the pitiless calculation she saw in Shrewd's any day.

The Ranger frowned. "Are you well, Miss?" he asked Sienna in a low voice. Her heart warmed that he was concerned enough to ask her that, but all she wanted was to get away as quickly as possible. She could not afford to make enemies of the Hamm family; they were much too powerful.

"I just want to go home," she whispered. The Ranger didn't challenge her or force the issue, he just led her away, casting a dark look over his shoulder to make sure the two men didn't attempt to follow them. When they had walked some distance away, he stopped and turned to her.

"You're safe now," he reassured her. Sienna, still pale with shock, nodded then ran for the side of the street and violently retched. The fear and anxiety churning inside her collaborated to empty her stomach until she felt hollow. She felt weak and helpless and she hated it. No, she was not safe. What good was all the training she had been doing if she froze every time she faced an angry confrontation? Pathetic! When the dry heaves finally subsided, she looked up to find that the Ranger had stopped a carriage for her. She huddled into her seat the carriage, closing her eyes to wallow in her misery and inadequacy. The driver turned to look at her but wisely chose not to ask.

"Let's get you home."

~

SEBASTIAN FROWNED when he walked into the training room the next day and saw Sienna standing there in the dress she wore to breakfast. He had expected that she would take training even more seriously now he had agreed to take her for individual sessions apart from the other recruits, but it seemed she was going to blow him off.

"Why aren't you in practice clothes yet?" he asked.

"I am."

Sebastian took a deep breath to remind himself not to snap at her. He had misconstrued her intentions too often before to jump in now and assume he knew what she was thinking. "Explain," he commanded.

"I need to learn to fight in dresses. Most of my life I will be wearing them, so my movements need to be able to account for the limitations of attire, rather than assuming I will be able to wear more streamlined practice clothes. That would completely eliminate the element of surprise from using a female operative! Also, as a woman, I can't openly wear a sword at my waist as men do. So where and how I can carry and conceal a weapon will probably determine what type of weapon I can use, and thus what fighting styles and techniques I should be focusing on."

Sebastian was glad that he hadn't berated her clothing choice. Everything she said was valid, and none of it was something he had previously considered. For the first time, he realized that a female Ranger would have far more disadvantages to overcome than just size and strength. It was a fundamentally different concept.

"Well, it looks like we have a lot of work ahead of us," he said to her with a smile, enthusiasm bubbling up at the challenge. "Let's get started."

~

THE DAYS PASSED IN A BLUR. Mrs. Chambers helped customize Sienna's gowns, sewing invisible pockets into them and adding hidden slits in the folds of her skirts so she could reach weapons hidden underneath. Sebastian worked directly with her as promised, delighted in the new discoveries he made with her. Sir Marcus often joined them and occasionally even some of the Rangers would stop by, but Sienna no longer had any interactions with the other recruits. She was aware of mutterings of favoritism and suggestions of what she had done to earn that favor, but she blocked them out as irrelevant. She had come to Port Royale to learn to fight not to make friends; she was exactly where she was meant to be. For the first time in four years, she felt free from the shadow of fear that hovered over her; she knew she was safe here.

Devising a new training regime specifically for Sienna was such a distraction for Sebastian that he didn't notice the time slipping by. Suddenly, he found himself on the eve of Lady Camilla's arrival and he felt woefully unprepared. Oh, the castle looked wonderful and everything was ready, but *he* wasn't ready. The doubts and anxiety that he had ignored for the past few weeks came back full force. But he calmed himself by remembering that this wasn't some unknown lady; she had been specially selected and knew what she was coming for. Really, the visit was just a formality. The marriage agreement was all but certain already.

At a loose end, Sebastian decided to look in on the preparations by the castle staff, as he felt he had not paid enough attention to them or the great efforts they were taking to get everything ready for this visit. He looked in bemusement at the transformation that had beset his dining hall. The staff had been working tirelessly for weeks to prepare for Lady Camilla's arrival, and now it was time to put that work to the test as they put together the finishing touches for the Welcome Dinner. He approached Mrs. Chambers to check in on the status and make sure her team had everything they needed, but someone else got to her first.

"Mrs. Chambers, there is a problem with the seating chart."

To his surprise, he saw it was Sienna brandishing the chart. He belatedly realized she had been in the middle of the action all along, an oasis of calm amidst the bustle. "What are you doing here?" he asked her.

"She's my special consultant," Mrs. Chambers answered for her. "She's been helping me with planning this visit – menus, seating charts, entertainment, which guests should be invited to each event – all of it. What's the issue, Miss Sienna?"

"We can't put Lord Lucas and Lord Appleby at the same table. The two are still feuding over the comments Lucas made about Lady Appleby at the Ambassador's Ball last summer. Poor Lucas was only trying to look out for his friend by warning him that Lady Appleby was being indiscrete with Sir Colton, but Appleby was incensed at the slight to his wife's honor."

"The accusation was completely unfounded; Lady Appleby and Sir Colton were not involved in any way," Sebastian added.

"Of course not. Lady Appleby's lover is the Marquis d'Avenne," Sienna agreed distractedly. Sebastian looked at her sharply. *He* hadn't known that, and he was the premiere spymaster on the continent. "If we swap Lord Lucas with the Cadizan Ambassador that should fix it," Sienna said to Mrs. Chambers, referring to the seating chart again. "The new Baron Burtz is at that table and he shares a club with Lord

Lucas, and Lord Appleby traveled extensively through Cadiza in his youth, so he should be able to converse knowledgeably and fondly with the Ambassador."

"Excellent," said Mrs. Chambers, marking the changes on the master plan. "Thank you, my dear." She hurried off to inform the wait staff of the new table settings. Sebastian stepped forward to stand beside Sienna, and they surveyed the room together.

"How do you know about Lady Appleby and the Marquis?" he asked her quietly. She looked at him sideways and quirked a smile.

"Women talk," she answered with a shrug.

Sebastian was only just beginning to realize how true that was, and what an untapped market for information female gossip could be. Maybe he should consider recruiting more women to join the Rangers for infiltration and intelligence work. Speaking of which...

"I wasn't expecting to find you here," he confessed. "I thought this sort of event was anathema to you. I certainly wasn't expecting you to be leading the organization of the event with such skill."

"Just because I'm not *interested* in being a Society Lady, doesn't mean I'm not *capable* of it. I know which silverware to use for each course," she replied wryly. "I know how important this visit is for you. And after all you've done for me, I wanted to help ensure it goes as smoothly as possible. Everything should be perfect for the future Princess of Vitalia, because that's what *you* deserve."

"Thank you, Sienna," Sebastian managed, his voice choking up a little. She nodded in acknowledgment then strode off to adjust the placement of the floral arrangements in Camilla's favorite colors. Sebastian watched her for a moment, admiring the cool efficiency she operated with that made her seem older than her years, until he realized that he was getting in the way of others putting finishing touches to the room. He left to get ready himself; his guests would start arriving in a few hours, and among them was possibly the most important guest he would ever welcome to his home.

8

Lady Camilla arrived amid the pomp and ceremony one would expect for a Duke's daughter. Sienna hung back and watched her entrance, coolly assessing the new woman. She was definitely beautiful, artfully made up, and exquisitely presented. Her blonde tresses were coiled up on top of her head and her dress was striped brocade in teal and white. Sebastian stepped forward to greet her and welcome her to his home. Her retinue was also welcomed; the servants were directed to bring her belongings up to the suite that had been assigned to her and all her guests were shown to their rooms by Mrs. Chambers' underlings. Sebastian offered Lady Camilla some refreshments but she said she would prefer to freshen up first and so she headed up for her room, escorted by Mrs. Chambers personally.

When the entrance hallway had cleared, Sir Marcus turned to Sebastian with a grin. "Good choice, my friend."

"Sienna, will you join us for the refreshments?" Sebastian asked. Sienna smiled at him while Marcus rolled his eyes.

"Once again Sebastian, I think this is an example of

where it's best that I am not present with you. No potential bride wants another woman sitting in on her discussions with her future husband."

Sebastian flushed slightly. He was so comfortable in his relationship with Sienna he had trouble remembering that her presence could be misconstrued by others. He was getting too used to thinking of her as just one of his Rangers. He and Marcus went to the salon to sit and wait for Lady Camilla's arrival.

The morning went pleasantly. As it was a fine day, Sebastian suggested that they take a stroll in the rose garden. This gave him the opportunity to be alone with Lady Camilla without there being too much censorship from the gossips and chaperones. She was a delightful companion, knowledgeable and engaging. She asked about the flowers they passed on their walk and while he could answer some of her questions he had to admit to his ignorance on others. He asked her about her own favorites in return. The implication was there of how she might remodel the gardens when she was the mistress of the castle. She smiled prettily and made some charming suggestions, and Sebastian reflected that she might be the perfect woman for him. He noticed her glancing at his cloak once or twice but she didn't comment on it, and for that he was glad. There was time enough for that discussion later. It was not as if she was unaware as to the reason he wore the cloak, but as a first impression, it was not something he wished to discuss.

True to her word, Sebastian saw little of Sienna during the day but he knew he would see her at the dinner that evening. He met with Lady Camilla outside the dining hall and escorted her in to sit at the head table beside him. Surreptitiously, he looked around for Sienna and was relieved to see her sitting with Sir Marcus and some of the Rangers so he knew she was fine.

For her part, Sienna preferred to stay back and avoid the other guests at this welcome dinner. There were far too many nobles gathered for her comfort. Though they were mostly Vitalian, the ambassadors from other countries were also present and there was always the possibility that someone would recognize her. She kept back among the soldiers and the servants trying to maintain as low a profile as possible. The last thing she needed was her parents getting wind of where she was and attempting to force her home just when she was making progress with her training.

Sienna spent the dinner covertly watching the other guests for signs of trouble or acrimony. Mostly this was just to ensure that Sebastian's dinner went well and there was nothing to mar Lady Camilla's impressions of him and his home, but there was a small part of her – the curious analytical part – that was watching for signs of the next trouble brewing and gossip that would later make the rounds. Overall the dinner was one of tension for her, between her constant vigilance on Sebastian's behalf and on her own, and she was glad when it finished.

The guests were ushered into the drawing-room following the meal. Sebastian had a surprise he wanted to unveil. Knowing of Camilla's love of the harpsichord, he had ordered one especially for her as he didn't have one in the castle already. It had arrived only the day before. She admired the instrument and the thoughtfulness behind it, and after modestly demurring first, she agreed to play for them all.

Sienna kept to the back of the room not wanting to draw attention to herself but she listened avidly to Camilla's playing. There was no doubt that she was good. Her technique, her poise, her performance were all very polished and spoke to years of training and dedication. But Sienna had been to many recitals in her time and she noticed something lacking. There was a coldness to Lady Camilla's performance as if she played by rote and not from the heart. However, none of the other guests seemed to be aware of it or, if they were, it did not dim their appreciation of her performance. They clapped loudly and praised her effusively. Though Lady Camilla took the praise with an outwardly modest deferment, Sienna watching closely could see the pride underneath that said Camilla thought such praise was her due. *But*, Sienna reflected, *being proud of your accomplishments is not a crime.* In all other regards, Lady Camilla seemed to be a perfect fit for Sebastian and Sienna retired to bed that night happy in the knowledge that her friend had finally found someone worthy of him.

SIENNA'S good opinion was severely tested a few days later when the sound of shouting and a slamming door drew her to the corridor outside Lady Camilla's rooms. She found two housemaids in tears and Mrs. Chambers glaring at the door, red in the face

"What's going on?" Sienna asked.

"That woman," Mrs. Chambers spluttered.

"You don't like her?" Sienna asked surprised.

"Nothing is good enough for her," Mrs. Chambers fumed. "Always demanding, always complaining. She has the staff tearing their hair out, and now she insisted we take that painting down from her room because, and I quote, 'how do you expect me to look at childish scribbles for the next fortnight?'"

Sienna looked at the painting in question, held between the two housemaids.

"Is that a Günter Morova?" she asked in awe. The Nouveau Dessin style could be considered childish, she supposed, but there was hidden artistry to it also. Personally, she had always loved the color and simplicity of it.

"Yes," said Mrs. Chambers. "And it is the Dowager Queen's favorite. Sebastian had it put in Lady Camilla's room especially. He will be so upset when he sees it's gone."

"Well, it's not like he's going to be in her room to notice," said Sienna slyly. "At least not for a few months anyway."

"Oh," said Mrs. Chambers, her face clearing. "I see what you mean."

"Just put it out of the way where he can't see it and you don't have to mention it," Sienna suggested. "You can put it in my room if you like."

"Thank you, Miss Sienna, we'll do that. Girls," Mrs. Chambers called to the housemaids. They bustled down the corridor carrying the picture between them and headed for Sienna's rooms.

Just then, the door to Lady Camilla's suite opened and the lady herself stepped out. She looked surprised to see Sienna and gave her a cool appraisal.

"Who are you?" she asked imperiously.

"Carissa Antonella," Sienna replied.

"And what are you doing here?"

"I live here," Sienna said simply. "I'm training with Sebastian to join the Rangers."

"'Sebastian,' is it?" Camilla asked archly. "I see how it is. Well, the first thing I'll do when I marry Prince Sebastian is to put an end to that. Ranger indeed. I'll not have any of that going on when I am Mistress of this castle. You best find somewhere else to get your 'training.'"

"I'm not sure what you're implying Lady Camilla, but I

assure you there is nothing untoward going on between myself and Sebastian."

"And yet you call him by his given name," she sneered.

"All the Rangers are on a first-name basis," Sienna replied through gritted teeth.

"Yes," Camilla said condescendingly. "The Rangers. I can see how you'd fit in there. Well enjoy your 'Ranger training'; it won't last past the wedding."

With that, she pushed past Sienna and flounced down the corridor Sienna took a deep breath to stop saying something that Sebastian would regret. She couldn't help what other people would think but she didn't have to make the situation worse for him. She retired to her room to avoid further confrontations as she wasn't certain she could remain civil if she saw Camilla again that day and took pleasure in admiring the 'childish scribbles' of one of the greatest masters of the Nouveau Dessin style that now graced her wall. For all her education and refinement, Lady Camilla still couldn't appreciate beauty in unconventional forms.

9

Sebastian was on his way to the stables to meet Lady Camilla for an afternoon's riding when the sound of the harpsichord caught his attention. He followed it to the salon where, to his surprise, it wasn't Camilla at the instrument but Sienna. She hadn't noticed him yet, so he watched her from the doorway. She clearly had extensive training, she was completely comfortable sitting there playing. It wasn't as technically challenging a piece as Camilla had performed the night she arrived, but Sienna infused it with an expression that Camilla's more precise performance had lacked. It always surprised Sebastian to see this side of Sienna. He had gotten so used to thinking of her as part of the Rangers that he forgot her upbringing had focused on more traditional female accomplishments.

Sebastian entered the room and stood beside the harpsichord. Sienna kept playing with only a small smile to acknowledge his presence, showing she hadn't been as unaware of his observation as he had thought.

"I haven't seen you in a few days," Sebastian began.

"I've been deliberately keeping a low profile," she

replied with a shrug. "I didn't want to give the gossips any more fuel."

Sebastian bristled. "Has someone said something?"

"They've been saying it since the day I arrived at the castle. Everyone assumes I'm your mistress. I don't care what they say about me; their opinions are not important. But I won't let them malign your character in the process, or let ill-informed rumors sabotage your chances of confirming your engagement to Lady Camilla. She dislikes me enough as it is."

"Why do you say that?"

"Let's just say she has made it clear that once she moves into the castle that I will be moving out and leave it at that."

"She has no right –"

"Sebastian, leave it, it's fine. I can see where she is coming from, even if it is misinformed. I'm not going to be a source of friction between you two. I just want you to be happy. You deserve that."

"Happy doesn't come into it. I need to be married."

"Doesn't mean you need to be miserable."

"I'm not miserable, I'm annoyed. Why would Camilla be jealous of *you*? Why would anyone doubt your purpose here? It's not like we've kept it a secret."

"They can't reconcile themselves to the idea of a woman being a Ranger, and even if they could get past that, they don't believe *I* am Ranger material. The curse of my face, I guess."

"A curse?" Sebastian asked coldly. "*You* are beautiful. What would you know of being cursed?"

"Beauty is its own curse, if it hides the truth. I have been overlooked and underestimated my whole life because people never bother to see further than my beauty. My father looks at me and sees a damsel in need of protection. My fiancé sees an ornament with no opinions worth listening to. Lady Camilla sees a threat, because why else would a beautiful girl be in the home of a prince other than to snare a husband? Even you, you didn't believe I was serious about the Rangers when I came here. Even after I beat Marcus you still dismissed me as a waste of your time. I have to prove myself over and over because people look at my face and make assumptions. They think they know who I am without ever actually getting to know *me*. So yes, I would call it a curse."

"I've never considered it that way," Sebastian stammered, stunned. Who would have thought that a girl as beautiful as Sienna could understand his impotent rage at being judged based on his disfigurement? The frustration he felt when people treated him as if he were somehow diminished as a person because he was no longer perfect on the outside.

"The difference between you and me," Sienna continued quietly, "Is that I have accepted my curse and learned to work around it. If people are going to underestimate me because of how I look then I will use that to my advantage. Men will talk candidly to each other even when there are ladies present because they assume those ladies are so dumb that what is discussed will go over their heads. And women like Marie Jobert expect a pretty woman to care about baubles and fripperies. So I play to their expectations and win them over. Even though I can now hold my own or better in a fight with almost any man, intimidation will never be my strong suit. But infiltration and intelligence? That's where my 'curse' becomes an asset." She reached out to touch the edge of his hood. "How does hiding your curse help you?"

"Ahem," Butler cleared his throat from the doorway. Sebastian was paradoxically both relieved and regretful for the chance to step back from the intimacy Sienna's question had created.

"Lady Camilla is waiting for you at the stables, and asked me to find you," Butler said stiffly.

"Of course, the ride," Sebastian muttered, chagrined to have forgotten about it. He took his leave and hurried outside.

"I'M sorry to have interrupted you, Miss Sienna," Butler said in a pained voice.

"No apology necessary, Butler," she replied with forced cheerfulness. "Sebastian is going to be married so it is important he spends time with his future fiancée."

"I wish..."

"Don't," Sienna cut him off, and he nodded in understanding. They weren't the ones who would choose who Sebastian married. They were just the ones who would have to live with the consequences of that decision.

SINCE LADY CAMILLA'S ARRIVAL, Marcus had taken over Sienna's training. Though they worked well together, they both felt the absence of their friend. Sienna was parrying with Marcus when he disengaged and looked behind her. She spun round to see what had caught his attention.

"Sebastian!" He was still in his riding clothes, boots covered in mud.

"Lady Camilla decided she wanted a rest after our ride, so I thought I'd come and see how you were getting on," Sebastian said.

"I think we've done enough training for today," Marcus decided. "Let's order tea so we can just catch up."

"It's only been a few days," Sebastian laughed.

"A long few days," Marcus said.

Inevitably, talk over tea turned to the upcoming festivities surrounding Lady Camilla's visit. Sebastian asked if Sienna had sufficient dresses and she assured him she had, though she knew better than to bore the men with details of the gowns.

"What are you wearing, then?" she asked in return.

Marcus laughed good-naturedly. "What does it matter what he wears? His cloak will hide it anyway!" Sienna frowned.

"You can't wear your cloak to the Gala Ball," she told them. "It would be most undignified if the host, the most important attendee, was to snub his guests by refusing to show his face." Sebastian bristled, but before he could say something cutting in reply Marcus cut in.

"You know she's right. You can't hide your face forever. Are you planning on wearing your cloak on your wedding night?" Marcus flushed as he realized what he had just said in front of a lady. "Sorry, Sienna."

She laughed. "No need to apologize on my account. Sebastian, I understand you may not feel ready to reveal your face yet, but there has to be a better way than covering yourself with that cloak. What about a mask? It's something that you could fit just to your face and then leave the rest of you 'on display,' as it were."

Sebastian thought about what she had said. "That could work," he said slowly. "The scars are only on one side and don't extend lower than my neck." It was the most he had ever acknowledged to her about his scarring.

"I'm sure you could get a mask fitted to the right shape to suit you," she said.

"Yes, I think I could," Sebastian said, warming to the idea.

"But if you really want to make it feel like you've opened yourself up," Sienna continued, "get everyone to wear masks so you're not the only one. Make it a masquerade. Then no one will comment on one more mask in the mix, even if yours is a little more concealing than others."

"That's a brilliant idea, Sienna!" Marcus exclaimed. "But won't the ladies complain if we tell them now that it's a masked ball if they picked their outfits months ago?"

"Marcus, every lady has at least one mask in her closet that can be used for such occasions."

"Do you?" he asked curiously.

"I came here with one knapsack. Carnival masks were not top of my priority list for packing." Sebastian noted that she hadn't actually said she didn't own the 'masks that every lady owned,' just that she didn't have one with her. He wondered what that meant.

"It's decided, then," he said. "A masked ball it is." He left feeling much more cheerful, glad he had taken the time to reconnect with his friends. When he was gone, Marcus turned to Sienna.

"Do you really think Lady Camilla will be so sanguine about the change to the plans at this stage?"

"Absolutely not," Sienna laughed. "She's going to explode!"

10

"How would you feel about a field trip today?" Sienna asked Marcus a few days later.

"Sure," he replied. "What brought this on?"

"I just feel a need to get out of the castle for a while," she said darkly, casting a glance toward the gardens where Lady Camilla was walking with Sebastian.

"Not a fan of the future Princess?"

"Are you serious?" Sienna asked him in disbelief. "Or is she only supercilious and snide to other women?"

"Ah, no, you don't have the honor of being singled out by her behavior," Marcus put it as diplomatically as he could. Sienna snorted at his phrasing. "But Sebastian seems to like her and that is what matters."

"Sebastian deserves better than her."

"And yet she was the best available."

"I don't believe that. He's the heir presumptive to the most powerful kingdom on the continent and his sister-in-law is unlikely to ever have children."

"You forget that he is deformed."

"Don't you dare say that!" Sienna rounded on him. Marcus raised his hands in mock surrender.

"That's his opinion, not mine," he clarified. "He doesn't think he has anything to recommend himself as a suitor."

"Where did he get that daft idea from?"

"Princess Lacey," Marcus spat.

"Ah." Sienna scowled again. "That viper has a lot to answer for." She shook her head as if to physically dispel her gloomy thoughts. "Right, now I definitely need to get out of here."

"What did you have in mind?"

"Let's simulate an actual mission. I want to see how well what I've learned would actually hold up outside of the training room. You give me a 'mission' to accomplish – maybe to buy a particular item from some shop in town and deliver it to a rendezvous point – and we assume the mission is compromised. So a team of four Rangers knows which shop I am going to or the item I need to buy and they try to prevent me from making the handoff. And my test is to avoid or disable the spies if I can, and to defend myself to escape and complete the mission if I can't. What do you think?"

"Ambitious, but it beats sitting here for the rest of the day! Come on, let's round up some enemy spies and then I'll set your mission parameters." Marcus led her past the mess hall full of Rangers to his small office in the barracks. She sat down opposite him and waited impatiently for him to come up with the training scenario.

"Let's see. Princess Eva has a jeweled necklace on which the clasp broke the last time she was visiting. Sebastian sent it to Monsieur Lefebvre to be mended. Your mission is to retrieve the necklace and deliver it to me in Harbor Square before sundown. I'll give you an official letter, so Monsieur Lefebvre will know to release the necklace to you."

"Hmm, if I'm going to an upmarket jeweler's I should probably change my attire into something more in tune with his clientele. Otherwise, it won't matter how many letters I carry, he won't believe I'm someone who should be entrusted with jewels! But first, let's brief the rest of the team."

"Oh no, you don't get to see which four Rangers I choose, nor do you know how much of your mission they will know, so you can't plan your strategy based on that. Mimicking a real scenario, you know that your mission may have been compromised, but you don't know to what extent if at all, and you have to see it through regardless. Good luck; I'll see you in Harbor Square at sundown, whatever the outcome."

Sienna left his office with her letter in hand and headed to her room on autopilot, her mind already whirring with various options to transport the necklace without being caught. She got changed into her finest day dress, the one in plum and cream brocade, and donned a matching hat complete with ostrich feathers on the brim. It was far from inconspicuous, but she was aiming to hide in plain sight. She was sure none of the Rangers would recognize her in the outfit, so she just needed to blend in with the rest of the patrons in that part of town so they had no cause to look at her too closely. She looked through the jewelry that Mrs. Chambers had offered her the night of the Harbor Ball.' She put most of it on now – even an awful gaudy broach, that even as Lucia she hadn't wanted to wear – so that no one would think twice about anything shiny or sparkly about her person. Assured of this camouflage, she unwrapped the jewel-hilted stiletto dagger that she had brought with her to the castle. No well-to-do society lady would carry a sword, so she would have to arm herself in more subtle ways. She braided the stiletto into her chestnut hair. With most of the blade hidden, it just looked like a standard hairpiece, and she put her hat back on over it to obscure it further. She strapped a dagger to each thigh and checked that they were easily reachable through the slits she had cut in the sides of her dress, concealed by the voluptuous folds of the full skirt. She gave her ensemble a critical once-over in the mirror and, as an afterthought, added the glass beads that Marie Jobert had so admired at the Harbor Ball. She got into the carriage waiting for her as stealthily as she could. It would undo all the effort she had made with her appearance if the Rangers saw her now and could then easily identify her around the town.

~

SIENNA ALIGHTED the carriage in Place de la Marché. The broad square was devoid of the stalls that crammed into it on market days, but was still bustling with people, situated as it was between the Quartier Bourgousie and the Quartier Moderne, in the center of the town. The babble of voices, rising and falling in the cadence of haggling the world over, was accompanied by the shrill squawks of the seagulls who ventured into town from the port in search of scraps. From the smell of fresh bread, the baker had just taken a batch from the oven. She looked towards his shop and saw him shooing away the determined birds as he tried to set out his wares.

She took a moment to look around. Many of the newer buildings on the streets leading off the square were made of timber. Already evidence of the Magistrate's edict against the Hamms was visible. Three buildings on Rue des Poissons were cordoned off and were in the process of being torn down. Hopefully, the Quartier Bourgousie would be soon all stone buildings and less at risk of a fire devastating the town. The Hamm Bros. Construction Company might be poorer for it, but everyone else would be better off.

Sienna started walking towards the far side of the square. Ahead, Rue des Nantis, the most fashionable – and expensive – street in Port Royale gently sloped upwards, symbolically and literally rising above the rabble of the main market. The noisy clamor of the marketplace seemed to quieten as she walked up the street. Here, ladies and gentlemen strolled sedately. On Rue des Nantis, you walked to be seen as much as to shop. The buildings were three stories tall, but because the street was so wide, it didn't feel oppressive. It was a bright day. The sun gleamed on the cobblestones under her feet, worn to a shine by thousands of previous pedestrians.

She strolled along Rue des Nantis, pausing to admire the window displays as if she were any other young lady of means, rather than moving with purpose, which might make her stand out. In reality, she was using the large plate glass windows as mirrors and checking her surroundings in their reflections while appearing oblivious.

She spotted two Red Hoods as she walked down the street. Francois and Beaumont could have been on regular leave and not part of the assignment – they were wearing their uniforms so they were hardly inconspicuous – but she thought it best not to take the chance. She watched them surreptitiously in the reflection of the patisserie window and saw the way they carefully scanned each lady who passed them.

Got you, she thought, convinced now that they were two of the four sent to intercept her.

With two on the ground near the jeweler's shop, she wondered where the other two would be. If she was running the op, she would put one up high to give an overview of the street. Scanning the rooftops was harder to do subtly, so she looked at the shadows on the ground instead. A moment later she saw a slight distortion against the roofline and knew she had located the third Ranger. She kept walking, very aware of the two Rangers as she passed them but trying to conceal it.

Monsieur le Lefebvre's shop was situated at the crest of Rue des Nantis before it swept down to the part of town where the aristocrats resided. She walked slightly passed the door to the shop and feigned a double-take as if something in the display had caught her attention. She paused to admire it a moment and then walked in, hoping her charade would make the Rangers watching the street think that her stopping here was a spur-of-the-moment decision as opposed to the purpose of her visit to the Quartier Moderne.

It was cool in the shop, decorated in soothing blues, and the juxtaposition with the brightness she had just come from meant she had to blink a few times before her eyes adjusted. When they did, her heart sank; another Red Hood was already inside the store. She wondered if she could bluff her way through, maintain the presence she was a society lady interested in the bauble in the window and find a way to get Lefebvre on his own to retrieve Princess Eva's necklace surreptitiously. Perhaps Renaud wouldn't recognize her in her current ensemble, as different as it was from her usual attire around the castle.

"Good afternoon, Miss Antonella," Renaud greeted her with a smirk. *So much for that hope*, Sienna sighed inwardly. The smirk told her that he not only recognized her, he knew why she was here. He was definitely the fourth member of the Ranger team sent after her. They were taking no chances of missing her. She immediately set her mind to working out how to turn this to her advantage. After all, she now knew where all four of them were, so she should be able to plan an exit strategy to avoid them.

"Good afternoon, Renaud," she replied sweetly. "I didn't

expect to see you in a shop like this. Have you a sweetheart you are buying for that you have not told us about?" She was delighted to see her question had flummoxed him. The sales assistant had turned eagerly to him, ready to produce an array of bijoux for him to choose from. She could see the indecision on Renaud's face. If he allowed the assumption to stand, he would be bombarded by the clerk and would possibly miss what Sienna was doing. But if he denied it, the clerk might get annoyed at him being present in the shop when he was not a customer and ask him to leave, which would be even worse for his surveillance. He grudgingly submitted to the lesser of two evils and admired trays of bracelets, bangles, and other adornments arrayed in front of him. While Renaud was thus distracted, Sienna asked the other clerk if she might meet Monsieur Lefebvre, to discuss a commission with him directly. She was led into a private sitting room at the back of the shop and offered tea while she waited to meet the jeweler. He entered shortly after the tea arrived. He was an older gentleman but still sprightly, with a twinkle in his eye.

"How may I assist you, Mademoiselle?" he asked. "You are looking for special commission?"

"Actually no," Sienna admitted, handing him the letter Sir Marcus had entrusted to her. "I'm here to collect something. I think you'll understand, given the people involved, that this is a matter for discretion and so I asked to meet with you privately. There is a Ranger in your shop and he is not here to assist me, so I would prefer he did not learn the nature of our business."

"Of course Mademoiselle," he assured her, taking the letter. He scanned it briefly, checked the veracity of the seal at the bottom, and nodded to himself. "I will get the piece for you now." He returned a moment later with the necklace and a velvet pouch. Sienna looked at the necklace with appreciation. It consisted of several strands bound together at the clasp, and the craftsmanship was exquisite.

"Could you please check if that Ranger is still in your shop, Monsieur?" Sienna asked. Monsieur Lefebvre nodded and bustled out of the sitting room. While he was gone she stowed the necklace securely and was standing with the pouch in her hand when he returned with an apologetic look.

"I am afraid Mademoiselle that the gentleman is still there. Would you like me to evict him?"

Tempting as that thought was, Sienna knew it would just more problems for her, as Renaud would wait and ambush her the moment she left the shop. Instead, she turned to the jeweler. "How are your acting skills?"

RENAUD TAPPED his fingers against his leg, the only outward sign of his impatience and frustration he would allow. The jeweler's apprentice had a seemingly unending supply of trinkets to show him, none of which he was the slightest bit interested in. His interest was with the woman in the back room.

Monsieur Lefebvre had appeared briefly a moment ago, and then wandered off again, but still no sign of Miss Antonella. Renaud was starting to think that she might have slipped out the back entrance and was contemplating forcing his way behind the counter to find her, when the girl finally appeared.

Monsieur Lefebvre escorted Miss Antonella from the sitting room to the shop with all the attention and deference you would expect a tradesman to show toward a valued customer. Renaud zeroed in on a pouch she clipped onto a loop on her belt. *There's the target*, he thought smugly.

The would-be Ranger stopped suddenly, bracing herself against one of the display counters.

"Mademoiselle, are you well?" Monsieur Lefebvre asked in concern.

"Just a momentary dizziness, nothing to worry about." She brushed it off but she didn't make it more than five steps further when she pitched forward and landed on the floor.

"Mademoiselle!" The jeweler rushed to her side. "She's fainted! Quick, call a doctor! Get me some water!"

The apprentice hurried into the back of the shop, wringing his hands in distress. Renaud took an involuntary step forward toward the prone figure.He was torn between wanting to help Miss Antonella and the suspicion that it was just a ruse to get rid of him.

"You!" Lefebvre looked up and pointed at him. "There is a doctor in Place de la Marché – fetch him here quickly. *Vite*!" Renaud hesitated, but the old man sounded genuinely worried about Miss Antonella. Renaud was unwilling to take the risk that she was truly ill and potentially have to explain to Sir Marcus or the Prince why he allowed their protégée to come to harm through his inaction.

But if the doctor didn't say she was near dying when they got back, Renaud thought as he hurried down the street, he'd make her wish she was the next time he saw her.

Monsieur Lefebvre leaned over Sienna's prone body and whispered, "He's gone, Mademoiselle."

Sienna sat up immediately, to the great surprise of the watching assistant. "Thank you, Monsieur," she said to the jeweler. "You were magnificent." He demurred modestly, but she could see that he was pleased with her praise.

"Now what, Mademoiselle? Would you perhaps like to

leave via the staff entrance onto Ruelle du Personnel?" he offered.

Sienna bit her lip as she considered her next move. Sneaking out the back door wasn't an option, not with the Ranger on the roof watching for that. She thought about the building layout and the street. While the Ranger would have a good view of the alley behind this side of the street, he would have no visibility of the alleyways behind the buildings on the *opposite* side of the street. Leaving through the front door and crossing the street might actually be her best option. With such close surveillance, it was probably better if she wasn't waiting around the harbor for Marcus to show at sunset, but to arrive just on time for the handoff. She gave a little evil grin. *Time to take the boys shopping.*

"Thank you, Monsieur, but that won't be necessary," she replied to Monsieur Lefebvre. With a small smile still tugging at her lips, she sailed out the door onto Rue des Nantis.

Marie Jobert had shown Lucia di Constanza all of the key spots of the shopping districts for the well-to-do. Sienna was glad of that experience now, as she took her time visiting the tea-rooms, the milliners, and the drapers, always ensuring she was surrounded by enough people that the Rangers couldn't get to her without making a scene. She was relying on their desire for discretion to protect her until it was time for her rendezvous. In the back of the seamstress' shop, out of sight of her shadows for a moment, Sienna told the attendant that she needed to see the doctor. The woman nodded in understanding and directed her to a staircase carefully hidden behind some bales of material. Sienna slipped through and made her way upstairs.

Marie had told her that there was a doctor who worked above the seamstress' who could give a tonic to prevent pregnancy. As such a service needed to be discrete, the entrance was located in an area where women were expected to spend a long time. Their absence would not draw curiosity or suspicion if the men assumed they were admiring dresses. Sienna had no need of such services; the benefit to her today was that the upper floors of several buildings were linked together for the doctor's rooms, and the male Rangers were unlikely to know anything about this place. She went down the corridor as far as she could and took the stairs back to the street level about six houses down from where she had entered the dress shop. She looked out the front door: Renaud, Francois, and Beaumont were still further up the street and she could see Jacques on the roof opposite. Satisfied she knew where all the players were, she slipped out the back door and made her way toward the harbor via the smaller side roads.

Time to ace this test, she thought with a grin.

11

Sienna was feeling very pleased with herself and perhaps she was a little complacent because of it. She certainly hadn't maintained vigilance about her surroundings, because she suddenly found herself grabbed from behind by strong arms wrapped around her.

"Got you," a gruff voice in her ear said.

She struggled against him futilely as he whistled for his friends to join him. How had one of them managed to overtake her? She was sure she had left them behind on Rue des Nantis. The sound of running feet made her look up. She stared in confusion as she counted four Red Hoods approaching. The one holding her must have noticed her shock because he smirked at her. "What's wrong, were you only expecting four?"

Sienna realized that she had made the cardinal mistake of assuming that Marcus had given her total information. She had known that the brief the Rangers would get would be limited, but never considered that her information about her opposition could be equally compromised.

"Well played," she muttered. She went limp in her captor's arms and stopped struggling. Assuming he had her compliance he let her go and she realized that it was Etienne. Feigning defeat, she slumped against the wall but surreptitiously she reached her hand through the slits in her skirt to reach the dagger at her thigh. While the other four were still some distance off she pulled the dagger out and held it to Etienne's neck.

"You're dead," she whispered with a smile. He looked at her in shock. Clearly, he hadn't expected that she would fight. When the other four saw that she had just 'taken out' one of their teammates they rushed her, all four grabbing her. In the scuffle, she dropped the knife and Francois and Jacques held her arms to stop her going for them with her fists. Beaumont opened a door in the alley and they dragged Sienna through it into a warehouse.

"Should she be patted down, to make sure she doesn't have any other weapons?" Jacques asked doubtfully.

"You want to explain to Sir Marcus that you put your hands on her?" Etienne asked with a smirk. "Or better yet, explain it to Sebastian?" Jacques blanched, which Etienne assumed was answer enough.

"You're dead," said Renaud. "You don't get a say in this game anymore."

Etienne nodded and raised his hands in acquiescence staying silent, but he grinned at Sienna as he noticed that Renaud didn't give the order to search her all the same.

"Beaumont, get the necklace," Renaud ordered. Beaumont looked at Jacques nervously then back at Renaud.

"Get it from where?" he asked hesitantly.

"Fine, I'll do it myself," Renaud snarled. He walked up to Sienna, stood in her space, and reached his hand round her waist to find the little pouch he had seen her attach there as she left the jewelry store. She looked up at him and arched an eyebrow, challenging him on the intimacy of the way he was touching her.

"Getting a little close there, Renaud?" she asked. Renaud gritted his teeth but didn't rise to the bait. He found the pouch and pulled it off her belt.

"Got it," he told the others.

"Are you sure that's it?" asked Beaumont. Renaud looked like he was going to snap at Beaumont but then thought better of it and realized that it was a valid question. He opened the pouch and poured out the necklace. Its strands glinted in the light of the setting sun filtering through the warehouse's one window.

"That's it," Renaud confirmed, putting it back in the pouch. "Now, tie her up."

"What?" Francois asked shocked.

"Well, we can't have her following us and trying to ambush us before the rendezvous. It's not quite sunset yet." Renaud said. "So tie her up to make sure she can't make it."

Francois and Jacques looked uncomfortable but they did as Renaud instructed. Sienna was sure that Renaud was only doing this because he was pissed she had made him look like a fool back at the jewelry shop. While she was not impressed with his tactics, she didn't want Francois and Jacques feeling guilty about following orders so she smiled at them as Francois wrapped some cord around her wrists and ankles. She even offered her wrists up to him to make it easier. In return, she thought that Francois had deliberately left her bonds a little slacker than they would normally do for a prisoner. He gave her an apologetic look and she gave him a smile of understanding in return.

"Right, let's go," Renaud ordered. Jacques, Francois, and Beaumont followed him out of the warehouse, presumably heading to the harbor and victory. Beaumont looked back at Etienne.

"Are you coming?"

Etienne shrugged. "I'm dead. I'm not obliged to present myself to claim the prize."

"Suit yourself."

Once the four Red Hoods had closed the door behind them, Etienne rushed to Sienna's side. "I'm sorry," he said to her. "They went too far. Here, let me help you get back to the castle."

"No, don't help me!" Sienna said. "The mission isn't over yet." Her cooperation with her captors had only partially been in sympathy with Francois and Jacques' predicament. Mainly, it was so she could influence them to tie her hands in front of her rather than behind her back. With her ankles bound as well, she was sitting at too awkward an angle to reach the dagger strapped to her left thigh, but it was a simple matter to raise her bound hands over her head and pull the dagger out of her hair. Etienne looked at her in amazement. Holding the dagger in her hands she first undid the bindings on her feet so she could stand up again and then more carefully turned the blade toward herself to saw at the bindings around her wrists. Her caution meant it went a little slower but at least she didn't cut herself. Etienne just stared at her dumbfounded as the cord fell away. Sienna grinned at him.

"Sun hasn't set yet," she said. "There's still time to meet Marcus and complete the mission."

"But how are you going to get the necklace back?" Etienne asked her, as she headed for the door.

"Oh," she smiled with a glance back at him. "I won't have to." Etienne hurried to catch up and fell into step beside her as she marched toward the harbor.

~

Marcus was furious with Renaud when the Rangers told him that they had tied up Sienna and left her in a warehouse. He snatched the pouch from Renaud and prepared to march away from the harbor in order to find her when the lady herself appeared.

"Sienna!" Marcus cried. "Are you all right? They said they tied you up!"

"They need to learn to tie better knots," Sienna replied. "Or at least to search the people they are tying up to make sure they haven't left any knives in their possession." Jacques glared at Renaud as if to say *I told you so* but Renaud was too busy scowling at Sienna to notice.

"You still lost," Renaud said nastily to Sienna. "We are the ones who got the necklace."

"Really?" Sienna asked sweetly. "Marcus, would you mind checking the contents of that pouch? Is that Princess Eva's necklace?" Marcus opened the pouch and looked in puzzlement at the necklace in his hands.

"This is Orellan glass," he said.

"Yes," said Sienna. "Thank you, that's mine." She plucked it out of his hand and fastened it around her neck again.

"Where's the necklace then?" Renaud demanded. "I searched you. You didn't have anything else with you."

"Oh Renaud," she smiled. "I'm *wearing* the necklace." She pulled back the ruffled sleeves of her gown to expose several strands of pearls wrapped around her wrist. "I believe this is the necklace you are looking for, Sir Marcus?" she said unwinding it and handed it to him.

"Indeed it is," he confirmed with a grin. "But may I ask why you are wearing a necklace on your wrist?"

"Because no man would look at a wrist and see a necklace, only a bracelet. Things that are hidden are suspicious and easily taken off you. Things that look like they belong are often overlooked."

"That they are," Marcus agreed. "Well done everyone. I think this training exercise has been a great success and thank you for your participation. Have the rest of the evening off. See you back the barracks later."

Etienne, Francois, Jacques, and Beaumont gathered around Sienna to say a few words of congratulations before they dispersed, but Renaud stormed off without a word. When the five Red Hoods had left Marcus looked at Sienna and offered her his arm.

"May I escort you back to the castle?" he asked with mock formality.

"I would be delighted, sir," she answered with a grin.

Sebastian had been waiting for Marcus to return, so when he heard the carriage he went out into the hallway to meet him. To his surprise, Sienna was also with him. She looked a little disheveled though she had clearly made an attempt to put herself back in order. Her hair was mussed and she was carrying her hat in her hand rather than wearing it. Sebastian looked between them wondering what they had been doing

"Where were you?" he asked, trying to sound merely interested and not accusatory or suspicious. He wasn't sure how successful he was.

"We went to town to get Princess Eva's necklace," Sienna told him.

"Monsieur Lefebvre had mended the catch so I thought it would be nice if you had it to give to her when she comes here for the Masquerade Ball tomorrow," Marcus added with a sideways glance at Sienna. He handed him the jeweler's pouch containing the real necklace.

Sebastian took it but scrutinized his two friends. Something seemed off here. Marcus had a vaguely guilty expression. Were they lying to him? But that *was* Eva's necklace. Maybe he was just being paranoid. Unless... Was Marcus courting Sienna? The thought gave him an unpleasant jolt. He was about to announce his own engagement surely he should feel pleased if Marcus had found that same happiness? Sienna was a wonderful young woman who would make a wonderful wife, especially as she understood the demands that leading the Rangers placed. And if Sienna was engaged to Marcus, Camilla would have no reason to see her as a threat anymore. Sebastian could keep his protégée and continue to train her. It seemed like a great solution all round. Sebastian knew he should feel happy at this development.

He wondered why he didn't.

12

Sienna entered the salon feeling self-conscious in her ball gown and mask. This whole scenario was a little too close to the life she had run away from for her comfort. It made her wonder if she had done the right thing and she hated self-doubt. Even though she was already wearing a mask Sebastian and Marcus had no trouble recognizing her.

"You look beautiful Sienna," Sebastian said as she entered.

"I could say the same to you," she replied. "It's nice to finally be able to see your face. Or at least most of it." Sebastian touched his mask self-consciously, his lips quirking up in a smile.

"It feels different," he admitted. "But in a good way."

"Your dress is lovely," Sir Marcus added. Sienna looked down at the dress with a frown.

"I'm not sure. I asked Mrs. Chambers for something plain in navy but I don't think she was really paying attention." Tiny crystal beads were sown throughout the midnight blue dress, winking like stars on the night sky. Marcus grinned. "I think she knew exactly what she was doing. And seeing as this fellow is already spoken for, may I have the pleasure of escorting you to the ball tonight?"

"Thank you, my Lord," Sienna replied with a curtsy. "I would be honored."

Just then Lady Camilla entered. Her dress was gold and yellow silk, and it was so wide she almost couldn't fit through the door

"Now *that* is an exquisite dress," Sienna whispered to Marcus. She noticed that the mask was a slightly different shade to the dress and snickered to herself at the inconveniences the impromptu masquerade must have caused Lady Camilla.

"My lady," Sebastian said bowing. "You look radiant."

"Thank you, Sebastian," she simpered in response. Was is Sienna's imagination, or did she put extra emphasis on her use of his given name?

Lady Camilla looked around the room. Sienna thought this was a bit pointless as it was perfectly obvious that there were only two other occupants, both of whom she ignored.

"Have your family not arrived yet? I thought they would be here to greet me," she pouted.

"Philippe and Marianne will be joining us momentarily," Sebastian assured her. "Princess Eva was delayed and is still getting ready, but I hope her tardiness will not affect your enjoyment of the evening?"

"Indeed no," Lady Camilla said smiling sweetly.

The door opened again and the royal couple walked in. Though she had seen him before, Sienna was struck for the first time by how similar King Philippe and Prince Sebastian actually were. Intellectually she had known that they were identical twins but seeing them side-by-side, without Sebastian's cloak obscuring most of his features, really brought it home to her how true that was. They both had the same brown hair, the same chiseled jawline, same aquiline nose.

It was strange to be able to see these details about Sebastian finally. Almost like looking at a different person. Handsome though the brothers were, they were both eclipsed by the exotic beauty that was Queen Marianne. Her dress was ivory satin trimmed in lace, which set off her dark skin perfectly. She wore pearls around her neck and braided through her hair around her crown, emphasizing her elegant neckline. She came forward to greet Lady Camilla, her future sister-in-law, and they looked like the sun and the moon standing beside each other. Though Lady Camilla said all the right things, Sienna couldn't help but feel there was an undercurrent to her words, a subtle sneering at the Queen, and she felt a wave of protectiveness rise up in her. Sienna wondered how much the Duke of Belgravia had been involved in the various machinations against Marianne at court. Perhaps Lady Camilla realized that she could supplant Marianne as the First Lady of Vitalia if she could beget Sebastian an heir while Marianne was still childless. King Philippe nodded in the direction of Marcus and Sienna and they bowed and curtsied respectively in return. But Queen Marianne came straight over to them when she had finished talking with Lady Camilla.

"Sir Marcus, it's lovely to see you again," she said warmly. "And you must be the female Ranger. I've heard so much about you," she added to Sienna. Philippe gestured for her from across the room. "Ah. Perhaps getting to know each other will have to wait for another time?" Marianne said with a smile.

"I look forward to it, Your Majesty," Sienna said with a curtsy, and she actually meant it.

"Shall we head for the ball?" Sebastian suggested to the room at large. He offered Camilla his arm and led her toward the door. Sienna didn't miss the slight smirk on her face as she preceded the Queen out of the room. Sienna and

Marcus stood back to let King Philippe and Queen Marianne go next, and they followed at the rear.

The King and Queen entered the ballroom to fanfare, as did Sebastian and Lady Camilla who entered last as the guests of honor. Sienna was keen to avoid having to be announced to the room and so Marcus agreed to enter the ball through a side door and thus avoid the Herald. Sienna was very glad of her mask. Looking around the room, there was far too much of the nobility gathered here for her comfort. Without the mask, she would surely be recognized and even with it, there was a risk. After all, if she could recognize Lord Lucas from across the room due to his potbelly and tall blonde wife surely others who knew her would equally be able to pick her out. Of course, no one was expecting her to be living in the castle. But then they might just think that she was a guest at the ball, and how would she explain *that* if anyone from the castle were to observe?

She made her way toward the staircase that led to the upper mezzanine looking over the ballroom. She took a glass of punch from a passing waiter and sipped it while observing all below her. Sometime later she was startled by a voice at her elbow.

"I was wondering where you had gotten to." Sebastian stood beside her. Even if she had not seen him earlier in his costume and mask, she would have recognized his voice anywhere.

"What are you doing here?"

"I'm not sure if you realize, but this is my party in my castle," Sebastian joked.

"I mean, what are you doing *here*, with me? Shouldn't you be circulating with Lady Camilla, or talking with some of the Lords, or something?"

"Ugh, don't remind me. Every backstabbing noble who plotted to overthrow Marianne has spotted the winds are changing and is now trying to curry favor with Lady Camilla instead. I am sick of the sycophants."

"They're kind of part of the job description," Sienna commiserated. "But if you really want to avoid them, just ask Lady Camilla to dance. I mean, before this night is over she will be your fiancée, won't she? So, shoo! Go, spend some time with her!" Sebastian took his dismissal with good humor and headed back down to the main ballroom.

SEBASTIAN WAS DANCING with Marianne some time later when he was roughly pulled out of her grasp. He turned around angry at the affront but curbed the sharp words on his tongue when he saw it was one of the foreign diplomats, the Orellan Ambassador.

"Where is she?" he demanded. "Where is La Principessa?"

"Princess Violetta?" Sebastian asked in confusion. "She's at home in Behr. She and Lord Albrecht declined to come as she is too close to her confinement period."

"Not La Principessa Violetta," the Ambassador spat. "Her sister. I know she is here."

"If Princess Olivia is here, it is news to me. Last I heard, she was chasing horses in Eddally and couldn't be contacted."

"And King Stefano informed Philippe that he and the rest of the family would be on vacation on Isola dei Fiori, which is why they would not be attending tonight," Marianne added, annoyed by the drunken man's obnoxious behavior. The Ambassador stepped into Sebastian's personal space and stared straight into his eyes.

"I know she was here, and I will find her," he insisted. "And then you will pay for this insult!" By the point, the altercation had attracted an audience. King Philippe, Lady Camilla, and her father, the Duke of Belgravia, had come to stand behind Sebastian and Marianne, while the Ambassador's wife and three diplomats from his Embassy had gathered around him.

"Let's go, Umberto," his wife cajoled him nearly in tears, as two of the diplomats led him away.

"I will find her!" the Ambassador yelled back over his shoulder. "My king will hear of this. You won't get away with it!"

The remaining diplomat winced with each word, and once the Ambassador had been removed from their earshot he apologized profusely for his boss' behavior. Sensing the fun was over, the rest of the crowd dispersed, and Sebastian waved off the diplomat's apologies.

"What is it you won't get away with?" Philippe asked Sebastian in confusion.

"I have no idea," Sebastian replied, equally confused.

"He was drunk," Marianne said with a shrug.

"A drink sounds like an excellent idea right now," Sebastian muttered.

"In that case," the Duke of Belgravia said smoothly. "May I take your charming partner?"

"And as our dance was interrupted, I claim this one as well, Lady Camilla," Philippe said to her as Marianne started dancing with the Duke. She accepted with alacrity, and Philippe led her away giving his brother a few moments of peace to compose himself. *Thank you*, Sebastian mouthed at Philippe behind Camilla's back, and Philippe winked in reply. There were advantages to having more of his face visible, Sebastian reflected, as he moved away from the dancing to the edges of the ballroom.

~

SIENNA GAVE Sebastian a look of exasperation as she watched him ascend the stairs to her hiding place again. "I couldn't take any more of those vultures," he offered by way of explanation. "And before you say anything, Lady Camilla is dancing with Philippe and Marianne is dancing with the Duke of Belgravia so I'm not neglecting any duty and I needed an escape."

"So happy to be able to oblige you, Your Highness," Sienna said sarcastically.

Sebastian took two drinks from a passing waiter and offered one to her. He swallowed his own punch quickly and felt better as the alcohol took the edge off his frustration. "And one of the Ambassadors just accosted me, and drunkenly accused me of I don't know what... and I was very diplomatic and didn't shout at him for his stupidity. Trust me, I have earned this reprieve." He saw the faint smile she tried to hide, so he knew she wasn't really cross with him for coming to hide with her. He watched her watching the dancers below, subtly swaying to the music, and was seized by an overwhelming impulse.

"Dance with me?" he asked.

Sienna looked uncertain so he took the drink from her and deposited it on a nearby table. He pulled her into a waltz hold and she didn't resist him. They moved effortlessly together. Sienna was very conscious of how close they were to each other. Sure, they have been closer during some of their sparring sessions as they fought together, but it felt different in this darkened alcove, in this secret place out of time. Perhaps the difference was also being able to look into Sebastian's eyes and see the expression there, the curve of his lip as he smiled back at her. There was something fragile building between them at that moment. She was afraid to probe it, in case it would break so she held his eye contact and let it expand between them as they danced.

"Sorry to interrupt."

Sebastian and Sienna broke apart, startled by the voice. Neither of them had noticed Marcus approaching them, which was very poor situational awareness from two Rangers.

"Lady Camilla is looking for you," Marcus said to Sebastian. "And I think the King is anxious for the two of you to conclude your agreement."

"Of course." Sebastian drew back. "Thank you for the dance Sienna, please excuse me."

He bowed and walked away. Sienna watched him leave with a slight flush to her cheeks, not quite sure what had just happened between them. Marcus cast curious glances toward Sebastian's retreating figure but wisely chose not to speculate about anything that the pending announcement would negate.

"Princess Eva would like to meet you," Marcus said to Sienna, as a way to move attention away from whatever had just passed.

Sienna looked even more flustered at this prospect. "Me? Why does she want to meet me?"

"She's been curious about the female Ranger ever since Sebastian told her he had recruited you. But this is the first time the two of you have been in the same room. May I introduce you to her?"

"I really don't think that would be a good idea, Marcus," Sienna said panic rising within her slightly. Princess Eva might recognize her. It had been many years since they had met but the memory was still strong for Sienna. She had to deter Marcus from this idea. "Lady Camilla is already resentful about my role in the castle. I don't think having Sebastian's sister pay me special attention at a ball in honor of Camilla would go down particularly well. This is a big night for Sebastian. I don't want petty jealousies or misunderstandings to spoil anything for him."

"I see what you mean," Marcus said. "Don't worry, I'll intercept Eva and steer her in another direction. I'm sure she'll understand. There will be another day when things are more settled when you two can meet."

"Thank you, Marcus," Sienna said with sincere gratitude. She watched him return to the ballroom and intercept a woman who had to be the Princess. She looked up toward the balcony where Sienna stood, but Sienna was confident that it was too dark up here for her to be recognized in a mask at a distance. She watched Sir Marcus lead Princess Eva onto the dancefloor and waltz her around the room, laughing and smiling with her. Sienna smiled at the closeness between them but her enjoyment of the moment was soured when she saw Sebastian and Lady Camilla leaving together. She knew Sebastian would be proposing to Lady Camilla and that then they would be announcing their engagement to the assembled company together. Sienna decided she had had enough of the ball for that night and unobtrusively slipped away.

13

Sienna didn't feel like going to bed just yet, too unsettled for sleep by the thought of the changes the soon-to-be-announced wedding would have on her life at the castle. She headed to the library thinking that a book might be a good way to pass the time while calming her mind, but when she opened the door she was greeted by the sight of Lady Appleby and the Marquis d'Avenne in the middle of a tryst. They were so enraptured with each other they didn't even notice her standing there. She backed out of the room and closed the door quickly, blinking as if that could clear the image from her mind. Glumly she realized that there would be couples sneaking off all over the castle to engage in similar behavior. Perhaps her room *was* the only place she could go where she could be undisturbed. But then she thought of another option. Sebastian's private study was one of the rooms that was always kept locked and no one would dare enter without his permission. She still had the key she had made to get into it the first night she met him. She decided that his study would be the perfect place to hide from the world for a few hours. He was the only other person who was ever there, and as he would be spending the rest of the night with Lady Camilla celebrating his engagement he would have no need of it.

She let herself in heaved a sigh of relief she locked the door behind her. This room represented comfort and security for her. She took off her mask and discarded it on the desk. She browsed Sebastian's bookshelf and picked up one of the few books not related to military strategy. It was well worn and clearly a favorite, so she decided that was sufficient recommendation. She stoked the fire and angled the reading chair toward it. She kicked off her shoes and tucked her feet under her on the chair, ball gown puffing out around her. She settled down to get lost in a book, in the hopes it would drive the current situation from her mind.

SHE MUST HAVE DRIFTED off to sleep by the fire because she was startled awake sometime later by the sound of a key turning in the lock. Sebastian entered his study and looked equally startled to see her there.

"Sienna!"

"I'm sorry, I shouldn't have invaded your space. I wasn't expecting you to leave the party so early. I thought you and Camilla would be celebrating into the wee hours." The words tumbled over each other in her haste to explain. He waved a hand at her, dismissing her concerns. She sank back into the chair and watched as he headed straight for the drinks cabinet.

"There is nothing to celebrate. There will be no engagement announcement. Lady Camilla will be leaving Port Royale tomorrow and there are no plans for her to return."

"I'm so sorry, Sebastian. I can't believe she refused you."

"Actually, Camilla was willing to go through with the marriage," Sebastian said, knocking back a tumbler of whiskey in a single gulp. "I was the one who said no. I realized I couldn't bear to bind myself to a woman who flinches every time she looks at my uncovered face."

"You took off your mask?"

"Yes, and she suggested I never do so again. In fact, she was quite vehement about it. Blast it all! First Lacey, now Camilla. Am I destined to be rejected by every eligible lady because of this cursed face? Perhaps I *should* propose to Princess Olivia!"

"Olivia?" Sienna was shocked by the suggestion. "But she doesn't like men."

"So I wouldn't have to take it personally when she shows no interest in me," Sebastian quipped in reply. "I thought I could bribe her to accept my proposal with horses."

"I don't think there are enough horses in the world to induce her to give up her independence by getting married."

"It was just a thought." Sebastian gave a defeated shrug. "The fact remained that I am still single. Philippe has already started to contact other potential brides. Despite the disaster of this visit, he will keep sending suitors to me. And while I'm wasting my time entertaining these ladies, the Ranger workload is growing. There is only so much I can delegate to Marcus. But Philippe is desperate for me to get married, so the farce won't stop until I pick one of them. I don't know how many more rounds of rejection I can endure."

He trailed off and stared at the fire in silent contemplation. Had he looked at Sienna, he would have seen her biting her lip, a sure sign of indecision. But she overcame her reservations and broke the silence first.

"So it seems to me that the only way to get Philippe off your case is for you to get married. But it doesn't mean that you have to do it his way. Why not pick a bride on your own terms."

"Like who?"

"Well, I could marry you."

"YOU?" Sebastian was shocked by the suggestion. "I thought you were against getting married?"

"Only to pompous jerks who think of me more as a possession than a person. But if we got betrothed your brother would stop trying to force marriageable ladies at you and you could get on with running the army. And I could continue training as a Ranger – nothing would have to change for us. I'm sure my father would agree to break my engagement if he thought he could get you as a son-in-law instead – what father turns down a prince?!"

"You're suggesting that we get married so that we can continue as we have been?" Sebastian said slowly. His world had just tilted on its access and his head was spinning. He imagined a future filled with evenings like this, sitting with Sienna and sharing his day with her. He imagined her holding their child in her arms, and he was seized with such a visceral longing that it was painful. "You know it's not just a wife I need, right? I need an heir too."

Sienna wouldn't meet his eyes and he saw her blush. "Well, of course, that's part of it, we would um, we could arrange that too." Sebastian didn't think he had ever seen her so uncomfortable. His heart sank again.

"Thank you for the offer, Sienna, but it wouldn't work," he said gently. "I don't think I could have a sham marriage with you."

"Oh." Sienna's shoulders slumped. "It was just a thought. Sorry, I've intruded on your space enough this evening. I'll leave you in peace." She left the room so quickly that Sebastian had no chance to reply. He wasn't sure what he would have said anyway. What she offered him was both perfect joy and abject despair. He didn't want a sham marriage with her, he wanted the real thing.

He sank into the chair opposite the one she had just vacated. When had this happened? When had his feelings for her changed from resigned acceptance to love? She had somehow snuck past all of his defenses and become necessary to his happiness. But what of *her* happiness? He had no doubt she would honor her marital duties, but he didn't want to be in her bed if he wasn't also in her heart. And her discomfort with the idea proved that was not on the table. What beautiful seventeen-year-old would love a man more than ten years her senior, and disfigured to boot? The only thing he had to offer was that he was a prince, and that was not a factor Sienna placed much value on.

And then there was the matter of her uncertain origins. Sebastian pushed out of the chair and started to pace the room, too agitated to remain still. Philippe wanted him to marry a royal, or at least a noble, to calm the discontent at court over Marianne. He would be unlikely to accept Sienna as a sister-in-law. Based on what Sebastian could piece together from what she had said of her family and circumstances, he guessed that her family was among the upper circle of the Cadizan bourgeoisie. Certainly, they were affluent, based on Sienna's manners and education. There was, of course, the possibility that she was part of the Cadizan nobility. More than once she had displayed an insight into the ways of the aristocracy that spoke of inner knowledge. But even if she was a Cadizan noble, it still wouldn't satisfy the court or Philippe. The court wanted one of their own on the throne, and if they couldn't topple Marianne then Sebastian's bride was the next best thing.

"No!" Sebastian shouted to the empty room.

He would not sacrifice his chance at happiness to keep those vultures happy. Philippe had married for love and made a common-born, *foreign* girl the Queen. Why shouldn't Sebastian marry for love too, if he could? He just needed to convince Sienna to love him in return. He laughed mirthlessly. There was little chance of *that*. But she was already a good friend, which was a stronger foundation than many courtships had. And now he had finally recognized his feelings, he was determined to court her. He just had to do it slowly and subtly, so he didn't scare her off. Then, when the time was right, he would tell her his true feelings and hope that she felt enough for him by then that they could have a marriage that was more than duty, even if she could never truly love him.

14

Sienna twirled in childish excitement, swishing her new red cloak this way and that. She had graduated from the trainee class and joined the Ranger ranks as a full member, including their iconic uniform.

The final testing for the Rangers had been a bit anticlimactic, truth be told. She had been nervous about competing against the other trainees. She'd had no interaction with them since Sebastian started taking her for individual lessons. Between staying in the castle rather than the barracks, and eating meals with Marcus and Sebastian rather than in the mess hall, she'd had very little contact with them before that point too. She didn't know their strengths or weaknesses, or if she could hold her own against them.

She needn't have worried.

It amazed her to see some of the trainees who had dominated the class in those first weeks struggling with what seemed to her to be straightforward exercises. The majority of the trainees outclassed her in terms of physical strength, but she compensated with skill. She assessed every test for the most efficient execution, so as to conserve her energy, rather than attacking each challenge with brute force as many others did. She was slightly disappointed that she did not finish the examinations in first place, though she knew that had never been a reasonable goal, but she finished solidly in the top quarter of the class. Her placing was more than enough to shut up her detractors and the lingering rumors of favoritism. Even Renaud had managed a gruff congratulations after the results were announced, though she suspected Etienne and Francois had prodded him to do so.

And now, the coveted red cloak was hers! She and Sebastian were in his study, as had become their evening routine. She was too giddy to sit still and danced around the room again. Sebastian smiled with her, her jubilation contagious. She pulled the hood up, obscuring her face in shadow.

"Now I'm the one wearing a hood and you are the one whose expressions are visible!"

Sebastian touched his half-mask self-consciously. He had kept wearing them since the Masquerade Party, perhaps the only good thing to come out of Lady Camilla's disastrous visit. Though he didn't seem offended by her teasing, some of Sienna's levity abated. She discarded the cloak so that her expressions were open to him again.

"Will you tell me about her, about the witch who did this to you?" she asked hesitantly. She thought he would shut her down but, after a surprised pause, he answered her.

"Her name was Alba. Other than that, I don't know much. I only met her twice."

"But I thought... Wasn't she in love with you? I thought she cursed you because your engagement to Lacey scorned her love?"

"Oh that was the reason," Sebastian muttered darkly. "It just wasn't *me* who scorned her."

"Lacey? *Lacey* and Alba?" Sienna struggled for words. "But... *why*? She was betrothed to you."

"Power. Alba was powerful, and Lacey couldn't resist the allure." He clenched his jaw in anger and it took visible effort for him to relax it again. Sienna hoped she wasn't doing more damage by pressing him to recount his story.

"So, what happened?" she prompted, quietly.

"Lacey likes people who are beautiful or especially talented in some way, preferably both. Alba was far from unattractive, but nothing extraordinary either. Her expertise in magic was what captured Lacey's attention. For a while, anyway. Lacey abandoned their relationship because she disliked being seen with 'someone so plain,' and told Alba as much to her face.

"Alba was devastated. She came to the palace in search of Lacey to beg her to reconsider, and she saw us together. It is not arrogance to say I used to be handsome – you only have to look at Philippe to see the evidence. The perfect picture we made together enraged her. She started shouting and screaming, hurling insults at us. Etienne and Trevi were on guard that night and they ran toward her with the intention of subduing and detaining her. But before they could stop her, she reached her hand out and curled it into a first. I swear I felt her nails rake across my cheek despite being on the other side of the room! And then the pain came.

"It was excruciating.

"My face felt like it was being seared, crushed, and grated, all at the same time. I fell to the floor, unable to stand. The agony was that intense. And Lacey just stood there, gaping at me."

His tone was dispassionate as if this information was of no consequence. But his eyes... there was a glazed, hollow look in them that scared Sienna. She recognized that expression. It was the same one that she saw in the mirror for months after her abduction was over. It was the look of someone still caught in the trauma of the past. She reached out and grasped his hand, offering him an anchor to the moment. He looked at their clasped hands in surprise, and she saw him retreat from that hollow place and come back to her. He gave a ghost of a smile, understanding what she had done.

"If the witch wanted to punish Lacey, why were *you* the one scarred?"

"Appearances matter to Lacey. She is beautiful, and so wants to be surrounded by beauty. That includes people. A royal engagement is not like a normal engagement. It is a contract. And not just a contract between the couple, but between their respective kingdoms. Lacey and I were bound by a contract between Karjala and Vitalia, which should have been inviolable. Alba assumed that Lacey would be forever bound to a disfigured man. Only when looks no longer mattered to Lacey, when she learned to look beyond external superficialities and appreciate inner beauty instead, would my true face be restored.

"But that was a lesson that Lacey had no interest in learning."

Sebastian sighed and stared into the grate, lost in memories. Sienna didn't interrupt his reverie, remaining a silent witness to his pain. Her head was reeling with the news. She knew of Princess Lacey by reputation – spoiled, arrogant, and certain the rules didn't apply to her – but even with her low opinion of the princess, Sienna would not have imagined this from her. She had heard through reliable sources that Lacey had had an amorous liaison with a servant on her father's estate before presenting herself as a possible bride for Prince Sebastian. She didn't think Sebastian was aware that his intended had not been a virgin when they met. And though the hypocrisy of the different standards of conduct that men and women were held to grated on Sienna's sensibilities, they *were* still the standards. But whatever indiscretions were in Lacey's past before she met Sebastian, the idea that she had continued her pursuit of pleasure after they were betrothed made Sienna feel sick in her stomach. Sebastian did not deserve to be treated like that. He certainly should not be the one bearing the consequences for Lacey's infidelity.

She knew he wasn't finished yet, but also understood that cathartic confessions couldn't be forced. So she waited for him to resume in his own time.

"Marianne was the one who told me. Philippe didn't want to 'upset me with the details' while I was still in the infirmary. The Healers were treating me as if it were burns; it helped with the pain, but not much else. Less than a day after I was cursed, Lacey demanded to be released from our engagement and she had cajoled her grandfather King Maximillian into supporting her request. Philippe assured me that he was 'handling it.' He had the magistrates and the army ready to defend the contract. But Marianne insisted that I should have a say in it.

"I had hoped that I had simply missed Lacey in the fog of the medications, but I knew that was a lie. She cheated on me during our engagement, and when I most needed her support she had abandoned me. Why would I want to shackle myself to such a woman? Especially when she had made it clear that she was unwilling, and would only comply if forced into it. I have never forced a woman in anything, and her insinuation only enraged me further." The apathy was gone from his voice and his posture. Bitterness laced his words, but his anger was palpable. Sienna didn't blame him. She was furious on his behalf, and her powerlessness to do anything only intensified the feeling. Sebastian took a deep breath, regaining some of his composure. "Thank the stars for Marianne, giving me a choice. I told Philippe to cut Lacey loose. I had no interest in fighting for her.

“It was a week before the Healers released me. The pain was gone but the damage was done. Courtiers stared at me and whispered, or looked away in revulsion. I, who had been the prize catch of the kingdom, was now the pariah. Marianne was dealing with her own whispers, and she provided a lot of good advice, but I wasn’t in a place where I could accept it. I avoided Philippe. He was busy learning to be king, and it was too hard for me to look at his face and be reminded of what I had lost. Eva had been really unwell for a long time and my mother was still focused on her recovery. I felt so alone, like there was no one who could help me.

“Marcus was a pillar of strength throughout those dark days. I don’t know if I would have made it through without him.” Sebastian’s eyes softened as he mentioned his friend. “He was the one who suggested I get away from the Court for a while, and came with me when I decamped to Port Royale. He had only meant a short break, but I found the solitude a relief and kept extending my time here. Now it’s home. It was while I was here initially that I first heard that people thought Alba had been *my* lover. I was too apathetic to set the record straight. What difference did it make anyway? And exposing Lacey like that would have caused more friction in our already tense relationship with Karjala after the failed engagement. So, I focused on writing my books and leading my Rangers, and resigned myself to this new life. There is nothing I can do to change my fate. Only Lacey can break the curse, but someone fickle and faithless enough to run away from the consequences of their actions is not someone who will ever learn to move beyond her own shallow self-interest.

"So that's it. That's my story."

Sienna swallowed a lump in her throat. "Thank you for trusting me with it." She blinked away stupid tears. No wonder that Sebastian felt so ambivalent about marriage, so bitter toward women. Princess Lacey had behaved abominably and Lady Camilla's cruelty only compounded his conviction. No wonder he had been so horrified by Sienna's inept proposal. Marriage was the last thing he desired, and she had tried to take advantage of his situation for her own benefit, to avoid her own arranged marriage. Stupid, Sienna, stupid, stupid. She was so relieved that he had forgiven her for it. She valued his friendship too much to lose it now.

SEBASTIAN STARED INTO THE FIRE. It was dying down, he should add another log. But he didn't move. It had been a long time since he had relived his curse and its aftermath in such detail. Everyone around him these days had been there when it happened, so there was no need for explanations. And his family danced around the topic, afraid of upsetting him by reminding him of it. As if he could forget, with the evidence branded on his face!

He hadn't expected Sienna to ask him, though her directness shouldn't have surprised him. He found he didn't mind her knowing. In fact, he felt lighter having confided in her. There was something about her that made him sure she understood his trauma relating to his past more than most. Probably because she had her own traumatic past, though he still wasn't clear on the details of what had happened to her.

He broke out of his reverie and got up to leave. Marcus

was standing in the doorway watching him. How long had he been there? Sebastian had been more lost in his thoughts than he had realized if he had failed to notice another presence in the room.

Marcus looked meaningfully at the empty seat across from him. "Have you proposed to her yet?"

"Who, Sienna?"

"You're too smart to play dumb, Sebastian. Of course, Sienna. You're in love with her."

His protests spluttered into silence under Marcus' knowing gaze. His best friend knew him too well. "Okay, maybe. Probably. Yes. But just because I love her doesn't mean the feelings are reciprocated." That was the real sticking point. Friendship and compassion and understanding were wonderful, but they weren't love. "She hasn't seen my scars yet."

"So show her! What's the worst that could happen?"

Sebastian stared at him in disbelief. "You *do* recall Lady Camilla's visit?"

"Do you really think Sienna is like Camilla?"

"No, it's just..."

"You're afraid?"

"Yes." There were not many people Sebastian would admit that to, but his best friend deserved his honesty. "I don't think I could take being rejected again. I need more time to be sure that she's the one."

"Don't leave it too long, or you might miss your chance. Sienna came here to learn to fight and become a Ranger. Who's to say she won't go back home to Cadiza now she's completed both objectives?"

Sebastian's stomach lurched sickeningly at the idea. His reaction told him all he needed to know about his feelings, and yet still he hesitated to voice them. He needed to ensure her acceptance, complete his stealthy courtship, before he could make himself vulnerable like that again. Marcus stared at him, and Sebastian could see the judgment in his eyes. But it wasn't cowardice staying his hand, only prudence. "A few more days, that's all I need."

After all, how much could happen in just a few days?

15

The sound of screaming woke Sebastian. He recognized the voice as Sienna's and she sounded terrified. He jumped from his bed and grabbed his sword as he ran to her room. He had no idea how the assailants had gotten in, but they weren't getting out again and they weren't going to hurt her. He burst into her room, sword at the ready, but there was no one there. He looked around, but no one was hiding. The room was empty yet still Sienna screamed. She thrashed in the bed as if fighting an invisible foe. Her eyes were open but glazed. Whatever she was seeing, it wasn't in this room.

"Sienna!" Sebastian shouted her name but she didn't hear him. He threw his sword aside and climbed onto the bed to shake her. "Sienna!"

"Carissa Nicoletta Antonella," he said as sternly as he could manage. "You stop this right now! You come back to me, do you hear me?" His voice cracked and he held her close. "Please, Carissa, please come back." He repeated it over and over again while he held her. Finally, the screams subsided and awareness returned to her eyes.

"Sebastian?" she asked confused. Her voice was a hoarse croak.

"I'm here, Carissa."

"Sebastian!" She threw herself into his arms, sobbing. He held her tight, comforting her, still not knowing what terror had gripped her. As her hysteria subsided he became very aware that she was pressed against his chest, and that she was only wearing a thin nightgown. With no threat in the room to defend her from, it really was highly inappropriate for him to be in her bedroom in the middle of the night. Sienna seemed to realize that at the same time, or perhaps she just picked up on his unease, because she drew back from him and pulled the covers around her. They were saved from the awkwardness by the arrival of Mrs. Chambers.

"Your Highness! What are you doing here?" she asked in surprise. "Heard the screams, I suppose. I wager the whole castle heard them. Nightmare was it? Well, I brought you a nice hot cup of tea. Nothing like tea to settle the nerves after a bad dream, I always say. If you want company, I'll sit with you a while. No need for the Master to remain."

"Of course," Sebastian agreed hurriedly, not wanting to give the wrong impression about his presence in Sienna's bedroom. "I'll see you in the morning."

"Thank you for waking me," Sienna said to him, looking straight at him for the first time since Mrs. Chambers arrived. He could see her sincere gratitude in her eyes, and also something else. Something that looked disturbingly like despair.

"Any time, Carissa."

Her eyes widened at his use of her given name, but he left before she could say anything in response. It was only when he had returned to his own room and looked in the mirror at his disheveled appearance that it struck him. In his haste to reach Sienna, he had forgotten to put on his hood. And Sienna had not reacted to his scars at all.

~

"It's getting late, I'm going to head to bed," Sebastian said getting up from his chair. He looked at Sienna, but she made no move to follow him.

"Actually, would you mind if I stayed here a bit longer? I saw you have a copy of de Trevet's *Philosophy of Peace / Wisdom of War* and I thought I might read it this evening." Sebastian stared hard at her.

"You're avoiding sleep, aren't you? Is something wrong?"

"No, I'm fine. It was just a nightmare," she lied.

"That wasn't 'just a nightmare.' You were terrified and I couldn't wake you. What's really going on here? Please, tell me. Let me in."

"I'm afraid, Sebastian," she confessed in a whisper, as he sat back down opposite her. "I'm afraid to go to sleep; afraid that if I close my eyes I'll be forced to repeat my ordeal, and I can't go through that again.

"I told you that I wanted to train with you because of something bad that happened to me. For you to understand, I need to tell you about my past." She looked away and took a deep breath as if to steel her resolve. She turned back to him and began her tale. "Four years ago, I was kidnapped. But the truly terrifying thing was that no one knew it had happened. A rogue mage we called the Piper hijacked my dreams and pulled me into his Dreamworld where everything was under his control." Sebastian tensed at the revelation but tried to keep his reaction to himself. This was about Sienna, not him. But it infuriated him that she had been the victim of misused magic too.

Perhaps that was why she had understood his own trauma so easily.

"Every night, I and the other girls he captured were forced to play his sick games to power the spell he was creating, with no escape possible. We were prisoners in our own minds." The horror of that helplessness colored her words. She paused to slow her breathing and try to calm herself. When she started to speak again, her voice was little more than a hoarse whisper. "And while he was violating our minds each night he also twisted in a spell to prevent us from being able to tell anyone what was happening to us. One girl kept trying and the consequences were nearly fatal. Even now, with the spell long broken, it is difficult for me to speak about it."

Sebastian nodded. He didn't think it was the spell blocking her speech, just the conditioned reluctance to discuss the situation, and the natural reluctance to discuss something so personal and horrific. He didn't talk about his own curse and never looked at his face in a mirror if he could avoid it. Sometimes the hidden scars were far more vicious than the visible ones. He poured a glass of water for her from the pitcher in his room and offered it to her wordlessly. She sipped it slowly, reviving her parched throat. It was a delaying tactic, and they both knew it. But Sebastian was not going to rush her; Sienna would tell him when she was ready, and he would wait until she was.

"Last night, it started again." Her voice was stronger, but there was still a quiver in it. Sebastian swallowed the questions that clamored forward, giving Sienna the space to tell her story in her on time.

"I've had lots of flashbacks over the years but this was different. I was in an unfamiliar castle, but when I got to the end of the hallway there was a ballroom. All the girls who were prisoners with me were there, all looking as bewildered and frightened as I felt. And I panicked. I didn't see the Piper, but I didn't wait for him to find me. I turned and ran screaming from that room as fast as I could, lost in the labyrinth of corridors until you woke me up." It hurt Sebastian's heart to see how fragile and lost Sienna looked.

"I tried so hard to move past this, to learn to be strong, but I'm right back where I started and I'm so afraid." A tremor rippled through her. Sebastian didn't know if it was her impotent anger or her fear that caused it. He hated the helplessness in this brave woman; hated that he couldn't swoop in and fix it for her. But just because he couldn't slay this dragon for her, didn't mean he had to leave her face it by herself.

"Carissa," he said gently, deliberately claiming the intimacy of using her given name. He took her hand in his. "I'm so sorry for what happened to you. But you are not alone this time; I'm here." *I'll always be here for you.*

"If you are going to stay awake tonight then I'll stay awake with you. And if you promise not to tell Mrs. Chambers, I have something that might help stave off sleep." He went to his desk and pulled out a small pouch. He loosened the drawstrings as he brought it toward her. "Mrs. Chambers considered this a slight on her precious tea, hence the secrecy. It's called –"

"Coffee!" Sienna exclaimed as the aroma wafted toward her.

"Yes," said Sebastian, flummoxed and bemused by her unexpected knowledge yet again. But the novelty seemed to distract her, which was good. Anything to chase away that hollow despair and bring her some comfort.

He fetched a hidden kettle from a cupboard and filled it from the pitcher, then hung it over the fire to boil. As they waited for the coffee to brew, he ruminated on the domestic intimacy of the moment. What he wouldn't give to have this as his future, to share such moments with Carissa every day, to be able to call her 'his.' Awful though the circumstances were, he felt that they had grown closer because of them. Now obviously wasn't the right time, but he hoped he would have the opportunity to broach those possibilities with her soon.

16

"Last night, her bed wasn't slept in at all, and the night before that Prince Sebastian was seen sneaking out of her room before dawn. No wonder she looks so tired!"

"I'm surprised she waited so long to make her move. I thought she'd make a play for him weeks ago. But I suppose now is a good time when he's feeling low about that Lady Camilla leaving."

"Exactly! She saw her opportunity and she took it."

Mrs. Chambers overheard this conversation and rounded on the two girls angrily. "You two better learn to hold your tongues about things you don't understand," she scolded them. "Two nights ago *I* was sitting with Miss Sienna because she was ill in the night. The Master came to check on her and that is all. And her bed wasn't slept in last night because she was downstairs staying by the fire to be kept warm and under observation during the night. If I ever catch either of you spreading disparaging rumors about the Master or any of his guests again, I will see you out of this house. Without references. Now, get back to work."

The two girls hurried away appropriately chastened but Mrs. Chambers wondered how long it could last. Surely they weren't the only ones gossiping in the castle today. She hoped that whatever was causing Sienna to lose sleep was resolved quickly. Her precarious position in the castle was becoming untenable and spending her nights with the Master was only making the situation worse.

~

SIENNA WAS SLUGGISH DURING TRAINING, her tiredness pulling at her limbs. Marcus noticed and called her out on it, but Sebastian intervened. He took Marcus aside explained the situation briefly.

"Go easy on her today Marcus. She didn't sleep last night."

"Oh?"

"Get your mind out of the gutter. Something is going on with her. She's told me some of it but it's not my place to share. She is terrified to sleep so she forced herself to stay awake."

"You know that can't go on indefinitely, right? She has to sleep sometime."

"I know. But for today, be gentle?"

Sebastian made sure that Sienna ate well during the day, using sugar as a substitute for sleep and he snuck her coffee as often as he thought he could get by Mrs. Chambers. But when that evening came, Sienna still refused to sleep. She walked around the room trying to keep active as a way to stave off tiredness. Sebastian sat with her again even though the lethargy was pulling at him too, and made them both more coffee.

The next morning Sienna was bleary-eyed, ashen pale

and haggard-looking. Everyone who saw her was worried by her appearance. Mrs. Chambers asked if they should fetch a doctor to see her, but Sebastian said it was just a lack of sleep through her own choice, and no doctor could cure that. When he told Mrs. Chambers Sienna was actually afraid to sleep she surprised him by suggesting that he "Fetch that foreign muck you hide in your study to make that stay-awake drink." Sebastian agreed it would be a good idea, ruefully acknowledging that he had never been fooling his housekeeper with his hidden stash of coffee.

That night Sebastian was truly worried about Sienna. She was ill to the point of throwing up and yet she still fought sleep.

"This can't go on Sienna," he pleaded with her. "It's been over sixty hours since you slept. Your body is shutting down. You have to sleep sometime. *Please.*"

"I'm too scared."

"Sienna, you are the strongest person I know, the bravest person. You never shy away from a fight. You always find a way through. Why is this different? You're not one to run away from trouble so face it head-on like I know you can. Because you *can* defeat this. And I'll be here beside you. I woke you up once, I got you out of there. If I see you in distress I *will* get you out again. I won't let the Piper take you. Please, Carissa, you need to sleep."

"You'll stay with me?"

"All night. I promise."

"Okay," she capitulated. Sebastian's confidence in her pushed out her own self-doubt, and she knew she would be safe with him watching over her. "Okay," she repeated more firmly. They went up to Sienna's room together. Sebastian waited in the antechamber while she got dressed for bed and climbed under the covers.

"You can come in now," she called shyly to him. He positioned a chair beside the bed, within easy reach of her if she needed him, and settled in for his vigil.

"Sleep, Carissa. Face your fears. But know you are not alone."

"Thank you," Sienna whispered on a sigh, and finally closed her eyes and succumbed to sleep.

When she awoke, she was back in the same stone hallway where she had started the first night. She took a deep breath and steeled her courage, wrapping Sebastian's words around her like a talisman. She knew where she had to go, so she started walking toward the ballroom at the end of the corridor. When she entered, she saw the other girls gathered as before, but looking more traumatized in the intervening days. They were lost and needed a leader; it was time to step up. No evil mage was playing his pipes forcing them to dance, so they had time to work out what was going on.

"I hereby call this meeting of the League of Princesses to order," Sienna announced from the doorway. Everyone turned to look at her.

"Sienna!" Princess Natashya of Siverus ran across the room to embrace her. "I was so worried. I saw you the first night but when you didn't come back since we thought the mage had gotten you."

"I forced myself to stay awake so that I couldn't be pulled back in," Sienna confessed.

"Clever," Princess Eva complimented her. For the first time, Sienna was struck by how similar Eva looked to her older brother. She put thoughts of Sebastian aside, there was work to be done.

"Four years ago, we made a pact to help each other when we were stuck in this nightmare together. We never thought we would have to revisit our ordeal, yet here we are. So now, we need to work out what new spell has caused this and how to break it. We will not be beaten by this. We are the League of Princesses!" It was true, they were all royal blood, representing every kingdom in Fable. Even Sienna, who was Princess of Orella.

"Hear, hear!" someone shouted in reply, and the mood lifted. They gathered around Sienna. Though not the oldest, she was the one they all looked to for guidance, the one they trusted could get them out.

"First of all, roll call. Is everyone here?"

"I haven't seen Princess Odette from Bretonnia at all," Natashya reported.

"And Aurora's not here either," Princess Rosebud of Northaven, Aurora's sister, added.

"Could they be staying awake, like you did, Sienna?" Eva asked.

"Unlikely. To go this long without sleep would be almost impossible. And they wouldn't have known to stay awake unless they came at least once, so someone should have seen them at some point over the past few days."

"Could they be excluded this time for the same reason Princess Lacey was excluded four years ago?" Natashya asked delicately.

Princess Izabella gave an unladylike snort. "I am married with clear evidence of the fact," she said patting her rounding belly. "If virginity was still a requirement then I definitely would not have been called!"

They continued to make suggestions and suppositions. Sienna retreated internally and processed everything said around her. Suddenly, the pieces started to fall into place.

"Rose! You said Aurora's not here. She should be sixteen by now; what happened with the curse?"

"We don't know," Princess Rosebud whispered. "She

turned sixteen three days ago, but instead of falling asleep, she just disappeared. Mother and Father had a plan to break the curse and wake her up, but they can't use it if they can't find her. We don't even know if the sleep-spell took effect or not before she disappeared. She could be asleep and helpless and *anywhere*." Rose started to cry, and Izabella comforted her.

"Three days ago?" Sienna asked. "Aurora's curse hit the same night that we all first came to this Dreamworld?"

Rose looked at her, dazed. "I... yes, I guess so... I hadn't connected the two."

"But they are connected!" Sienna declared in triumph. "I was joking when I called this a meeting of the League of Princesses, but I wasn't far off. We made a pact to help each other, no matter what, sealed in blood. Aurora knew her curse was about to take effect and she must have reached out through that blood bond for our help. But it's a sleeping spell, so she's permanently in this Dreamworld now, so..."

"So she brought us to her Dreamworld also, the only place she could meet us!" Eva finished, catching on.

"So the bad man won't make us dance again?" Princess Bianca of Cadiza asked timidly. She was the youngest of all of them; she had been only three when the nightmare started.

"No sweetheart," Eva reassured her, oldest to youngest. "No one will hurt you this time."

"But if this is Aurora's doing, why isn't she here? Where's my sister?" Rosebud demanded.

"I don't know," Sienna admitted. "But tomorrow night we are going to find out. Dawn is almost upon us, so I expect we are about to lose our connection to this Dreamworld, but we'll meet back here tomorrow night –"

"Not like we have much of a choice," Princess Izabella interjected wryly.

"– and we will search this whole castle until we find her," Sienna concluded. "And when we find her, we'll find out where she disappeared to and how to break this curse and free her, once and for all!"

The cheers from the other princesses rang in Sienna's ears as the dream faded to black.

17

When she woke again she was back in her room, and the first thing she saw was Sebastian sitting in the chair beside her bed, exactly where he was when she had gone to sleep.

"You're here," she said in wonder.

"I told you I would be. I'll always be here for you, Carissa. Carissa, I –"

"Sebastian, before you say any more I need to tell you something. You know I have not been forthcoming about my background. I haven't lied exactly, but there are a few key facts that I omitted. I want to rectify that now; I want you to know who I am, all of it. You see..."

"Sebastian!" Sienna was interrupted by a shout from Marcus, who appeared in her doorway a moment later. He politely averted his eyes from her and tried to look only at Sebastian while he spoke.

"Sebastian, I know you ordered that you were not to be disturbed, but your brother as just arrived and he says it's urgent. He is by himself because he rode ahead of the main party to 'give you warning.' He's in your study; please come as quickly as you can. Apologies for the intrusion, my lady," he added to Sienna, offering a quick bow while still not looking at her before he rushed away again.

"Since when am I 'my lady?'" Sienna asked, confused by his behavior.

"Since I spent the night with you, I expect," Sebastian replied with a wicked grin. To his delight, she blushed pink at the innuendo. "I better go, see what Philippe wants."

"Sebastian, before you go, I need to tell you..." He moved to her side faster than she could track and picked up her hand in both of his.

"I am not finished with this conversation," he told her with a rich intensity. "I have every intention of finishing it but I do not want to be rushed. So let me get rid of my brother so that we can have the rest of the day to ourselves uninterrupted." He lifted her hand to his lips and placed a lingering kiss on it, without looking away from her face. He was delighted to see her breath hitch in response. "Why don't you get dressed then join us in the study? There is nothing Philippe can have to say to me that he can't say to both of us."

"Okay," Sienna agreed weakly, understanding the implication of what Sebastian had just said, even if he had not formally declared himself yet. She went to her wardrobe in a daze. If she was about to meet Philippe as his future sister-in-law, then she wanted to be sure she would make a good impression.

"PHILIPPE, WHAT'S GOING ON?" Sebastian demanded as he walked into the study. He didn't care if he was being rude; Philippe's untimely arrival had interrupted something far more important.

"A delegation from Orella is on their way and they are

not happy. They are accusing you of kidnapping their princess and holding her captive. They have declared that if she is not returned to them unharmed immediately that they will consider it an act of war and respond accordingly."

Sebastian burst out laughing, but it quickly died as he saw Philippe's face. "*Merde*, you're serious. They actually think I would abduct a woman? And a princess at that? Why?"

"Perhaps they thought that you had resorted to desperate measures in an effort to find a bride," Marcus suggested glibly. Both bothers glared at him.

"I mean, why do they think I did such a thing? Even if they believe it of my character, that is hardly sufficient grounds for such a serious accusation."

"The Orellan Ambassador said that he saw the Princess in Port Royale when he was here during Lady Camilla's visit," Philippe elaborated. "He said that she appeared anxious and scared as she hurried through town. He tried to approach her, but before he could, she was set upon by four or five Red Hoods. She tried to fend them off, but they dragged her into an alley. By the time the Ambassador managed to reach the spot where he had seen them, they were all gone.

"Everyone knows that you control the Red Hoods. So either they were working on your orders or you have lost control of at least some of the squad who have gone rogue and abducted the princess for their own, as yet unknown, purposes. Either way, the Orellans want answers and I don't have any for them."

"Neither do I!"

"What's going on?" Sebastian turned in surprise at Sienna's question; he hadn't heard her enter.

"Sebastian has been accused of kidnapping the Orellan

princess, and the Orellans are threatening war if she is not released at once," Philippe summarized.

"And I can't release what I don't have!" Sebastian fumed.

Sienna's stomach sank. Her past had caught up to her. "Sebastian, can I talk to you please? Alone?" Sienna asked urgently.

"Maybe it was another group pretending to be Red Hoods trying to frame you," Marcus suggested. "After all, it's not like the Ambassador identified any of them – he is basing it on the uniforms, and anyone could wear a red cloak."

"Yes, that's a possibility," Sebastian replied. "At least it might throw enough doubt on the accusations to allow tempers to cool and sanity to prevail."

"Sebastian, please, there is something I must tell you." Sienna's pleas went unheeded, and her anxiety rose.

Butler knocked at the door. "Her Majesty the Queen."

Marianne walked to Philippe's side, but her words were for Sebastian. "The Orellan delegation has arrived. Lord Axel Forrester is demanding to speak with you. I had Butler put him in the receiving room, but he won't wait long."

Sienna blanched and fell into one of the seats. "*Merde*," she whispered. She was out of time.

"Miss Antonella, are you unwell?" the King asked, drawing Sebastian's attention to her.

"What is it, Carissa? What do you know of Forrester?"

"He's my fiancé," she confessed weakly.

"That doesn't make sense. You said you outranked your fiancé. Forrester is the Commander of the King's Army, my Orellan counterpart. The only people who outrank him are..." Sebastian trailed off as realization dawned. "Are the royal family of Orella," he concluded in a flat voice. "You're her. You're the missing princess that they're looking for. You're the reason that we are on the brink of war."

"I never meant for this to happen! I never thought he would come here to look for me!"

"So what *did* you think? Was this all some sort of game for you?" Sebastian fired back.

"No! I came here to learn to fight. You know that. You know *why*."

"Do I? Or was that another lie?"

"I never lied to you."

"You're the princess of Orella. You told me you grew up in Cadia."

"I've been at boarding school there for over a decade."

"Is your name even Carissa Antonella?"

"My full name is Sienna Nicoletta Antonella Ekaterina di Orella. I told you, only my father calls me Carissa. It means 'dear one,'" she added softly.

"Where is she?" a loud voice demanded, as the door to the study was thrown open.

"I'm sorry, Sire, Lord Forrester refused to wait for you," Butler explained following him into the room.

"*Merde*," Sienna whimpered again, folding herself back into the seat. Forrester's attention snapped to her when he heard her voice.

"Princess Sienna! Are you well? Have they hurt you?" Forrester rounded on Sebastian. "You flaunt her in front of me. You don't even try to hide the evidence of what you have done. Do you really think your title can save you from the consequences of this?"

"Now, see here, you jumped-up errand boy," Sebastian retorted hotly. "You do not come into my home and make threats."

"This is an act of aggression that Orella won't stand for. How long can Vitalia prosper if Orella cuts trading links?"

"Oh, knock it off, Axel," Sienna huffed, infuriated by his posturing. She stood between them. "Sebastian didn't kidnap me. I came here of my own accord and I had to convince Sebastian to let me stay. Marcus can attest to that. I stayed because I wanted to, not because I was coerced. I didn't even tell Sebastian who I was until today."

"You expect me to believe that the Spymaster of Fable didn't know that he had the Princess of Orella in his house?" Lord Forrester sneered. "You may be gullible enough to believe that but I'm not. I don't know what he is playing at or what his endgame is, but this charade ends now. We're going home."

"But I don't want to go back. I want to stay here."

"Now Princess Sienna," King Philippe said, in what he probably thought of as his kindly, fatherly, voice. "I think it might be in everyone's best interest if you were to return to Orella straightaway and reassure your family that you are indeed well and that this has all been an unfortunate misunderstanding."

"Sebastian?" Sienna appealed to the person in the room whose opinion mattered most to her.

"You should probably leave quickly, Princess. I'm sure you and your *fiancé* have lots to catch up on." He turned away from her, so he didn't see how his words impacted her. his cold dismissal landed like a blow to her chest, and she flinched back from it. The confidence she had been building during her time in Porte Royale crumbled under the onslaught. She had been deluding herself, thinking she could be something else. She was a Princess, an ornamental beauty, and nothing more. She dropped her head, refusing to meet anyone's gaze.

"Come along, Princess Sienna," Lord Forrester said patronizingly. "It's time we were on our way." He swept out of the room expecting Sienna to follow him. She risked one glance at Sebastian, but he was still studiously ignoring her. Left with no other option, she trailed after Lord Forrester. In the hallway, they passed Butler and Mrs. Chambers. Sienna kept her eyes averted, but Butler reached out and intercepted her.

"Is it true, Miss Sienna?" he asked. "Are you really leaving us?"

Lord Forrester turned around at the question and knocked Butler's hand away from Sienna. "You dare to address her so informally?" he demanded pompously. "She is a princess. You may address her as 'Your Highness.'"

"Axel, leave it, it's fine," Sienna muttered. Forrester ignored her. "The sooner I get you out of this place and back among your family and friends the better," he declared, linking her arm in his and all but dragging her out the door. Sienna resisted long enough to say goodbye to the heads of the household and to offer them apologies with her eyes before she was bundled into the carriage and whisked away. She stared out the window as long as she could. While she could see the servants standing on the steps watching her leave, there was no sign of the face she most wanted to see. Axel was droning on in his smug self-congratulatory way but she tried to tune out his prattle about 'rescuing her' and 'helping her to get home.' They say home is where the heart is; Sienna reflected that if that were true then Lord Forrester was 'rescuing' her from the only home she wanted.

18

The sound of carriage wheels on cobblestones faded. Sienna was really gone.

A yawning void opened in Sebastian's chest. He couldn't think, couldn't breathe. The shock paralyzed him. Sienna was a princess. A *princess*. She had lied to him. She had been lying to him since the day she arrived. What sort of game was it for her?

This couldn't be happening again! Why did every woman he cared for play him false? Sienna's deceit cut him far deeper than Lacey's abandonment. He had trusted her, and she betrayed that trust. *Her* betrayal cut him to the bone.

Anger seeped in to fill the void. The numbness was burned away by cold fire, leaving icy resolve in its place. He wouldn't let another woman make him her fool. He wouldn't pine for her. He wouldn't even *think* of her anymore. Love was for weaker men; he was better off without it. But he couldn't prevent one last yearn for what had been stolen from him.

Dammit Sienna, I trusted you!

~

Marcus and Philippe looked at each other. Sebastian still had not said a word or even shown any acknowledgment he knew they were still in the room. He turned around and rang the bell. Butler entered a moment later visibly upset, his usual stoic demeanor abandoned.

"Butler, please bring tea and some breakfast to us here, please. It's been a busy morning."

"Of course, sir," he replied with a bow.

"Tea?" Marcus shouted. "Yesterday you were planning to propose to that girl. Today, she is whisked out from under your nose – by Axel bloody Forrester, no less – and your only response is to order *tea*?"

Philippe gave a start at Marcus' words. "You were planning on proposing to the Princess of Orella? What a fantastic match!"

"Clearly, that is no longer a consideration," Sebastian told him coolly. "Princess Sienna has proven she cannot be trusted. I have had enough of liars and deceitful women in my life. I won't be made a fool of again." Butler arrived with the tea trolley and set it up unobtrusively while Sebastian continued. "So as I am still in need of a wife, can you select some candidates please, Philippe? No need to run them by me; you know my preferences, I'm sure you can identify someone suitable. Just let me know when to expect them so I can have everything ready for the visit."

"That's it?" Marcus blurted out, infuriated. "You're just going to forget about Sienna? Sit back and do nothing while you wait for Philippe to send you more potential brides?"

"No, I won't be doing 'nothing,'" Sebastian replied composedly. "One thing I have learned from all of this is that there is untapped potential in using women as spies. It seems they can infiltrate anywhere without arousing suspicion. I definitely want to pursue that further." He paused. "Of course, the difficulty is that the women most physically suited for espionage are the least able to defend themselves, and those with the physique to be fighters are not able to blend unobtrusively into social settings. It is something I'll have to ponder to find the best balance between soldier and spy for future female Rangers."

"I wish you luck with that," Marcus said standing up, disgusted. He strode out of the room and barely refrained from slamming the door behind him. He stood for a moment in the corridor outside to calm himself. He was still reeling from the revelations about Sienna and fuming at Sebastian's indifferent treatment of her. The door to the study opened again and King Philippe and Queen Marianne joined him in the corridor.

"I would never have believed it of him!" Marcus said, outranged. "He's behaving like... like..."

"Like a man who has had his heart broken," Marianne finished for him, taking the wind out of his sails.

"You think so?"

"Walk with us, Marcus?" the King suggested in reply. Marcus fell into step beside them.

"He found someone who could make him happy," Marianne continued. "But there is a voice inside telling him that he doesn't *deserve* happiness. That his disfigurement makes him unworthy of the love of a woman he can trust. Princess Lacey and Lady Camilla both lied to him – fawned on him in public, but when it mattered they both refused to accept him as he is.

"How do you think he felt when he found out that the woman he wants to marry has been lying to him for months as well? That the woman he fell in love with might not even exist in reality? And to have his nose rubbed in it by Forrester, his rival for nearly a decade? It's like the universe just slapped him in the face and reinforced all his fears that he will never find a wife he can love and trust."

"Was he truly thinking of proposing to her?" Philippe asked.

Marcus nodded. "I was expecting it any day now for the past two weeks. Ironically, I think he was worried that you wouldn't approve of the match. He really had no idea who she was."

"What about her? Would she have accepted?"

"I think so, yes. She's not like Princess Lacey. From the very start, she appreciated his worth and respected and valued him for more than just a title and his appearance."

"Did he know she was already betrothed to someone else?"

"Yes, we both did. It was the reason she wanted to become a Ranger, so she could get out of her unwanted arranged marriage. Of course, we didn't know that it was a *royal* engagement. Or that her fiancé was Axel Forrester."

"Do you think there's any chance they might still...?"

"You heard him, Philippe. He has decided to 'move on' and he is stubborn enough to stay the course even if it makes him miserable."

Marianne laid a comforting hand on her husband's arm. "Sometimes, people need to travel alone to mute the voices in their heads, before they can find their way home again."

"By the time he 'finds his way home,' as you put it, it will be too late," Marcus grumbled. "Forrester is not going to wait long to make Sienna his wife. Sebastian might find he has no home to return to. There is only one person who has any hope of talking sense into him now."

"Eva?"

"Eva."

~

THE SHIP WAS DOCKED in the harbor. Sienna's heart sank further when she saw it because there was nothing discreet about it. This was the Royal Yacht and it screamed its importance to everyone around it. Forrester kept a firm grip of her arm as he escorted her aboard, to the cheering of the passengers awaiting them. Sienna couldn't help feeling that Forrester valued her more as a living symbol of his victory over the Wolf the West than as a person in her own right. The passengers applauded Forrester and fussed over Sienna. They asked over and over again if she was all right, and expressed concern over the ordeal she had suffered. None of them listened when she tried to tell them that she had been in Port Royale by choice. Despite it being the Royal Yacht, neither of her parents were on board. She hadn't really expected them to be there, but it was still a disappointment to know that there was no one she could appeal to.

At the end of the line of well-wishers, she was engulfed by three ladies-in-waiting. They were not hers, but she recognized them; all were among her mother's trusted inner circle. They quickly bustled her off to her cabin – the liner's stateroom – to get changed. Apparently, her fashion choices as a Ranger were not appropriate for a Princess. They stripped her of the gown she had so carefully selected that morning to make a favorable impression on King Philippe and redressed her in brocade and satin. Once her hair was teased and combed, and strands of Orellan glass were strewn around her neck, the ladies decided that she was ready to go. They shepherded her back onto the main deck, where Port Royale was already disappearing in the distance as the sails were let out and caught the wind. Sienna strained her eyes to see it but then deliberately turned away. It was all in the past now; Port Royale held nothing for her anymore. As she stood on the deck contemplating this, the Ambassador approached her.

"Your Highness, I am so relieved that you have been returned to us, safe and well," he said with a bow. "I was so worried when I saw you being attacked by those Red Hoods in Place de la Mer! I tried to help you but you disappeared. And when the Wolf had the audacity to deny it all, I was truly concerned for your safety. But thankfully, Lord Forrester responded quickly when he received my message, else I fear what might have happened to you."

"You were the one who revealed my whereabouts to Axel and my parents?"

"*Si*. So it was important to me to be one of the party seeing you safely home, to reassure myself you really are well after all you've been through, *Principessa*. I can return to Vitalia and my duties at the Embassy there at the end of the week."

Sienna nodded vaguely, but she was too incensed to listen to his words. This was the interfering busy-body who had cost her the life she had built for herself in Port Royale! True, that life was founded on a lie of omission, but she had been about to tell Sebastian the truth and she thought he might have been able to accept it if it wasn't for Axel barging in and stomping all over everything. She pasted a false smile on her face, offered some banal pleasantries to the Ambassador, and excused herself as quickly as politely possible. The ladies-in-waiting swept her off again, but her smile didn't falter. This was what she called her 'court face,' the mask she cultivated to meet her father's expectations of what a daughter should enjoy doing, even if the activity actually held no interest for her.

But this is who I am, she reminded herself. *I'm a princess. Time to stop pretending that I can be something else.*

The day dragged on.

Sienna was glad to finally shut her cabin door when evening came and escape the constant clamoring and fawning of her traveling party. She was emotionally overwrought, still in shock at how coldly Sebastian had treated her that morning when an hour previously she thought he was about to propose. She couldn't make sense of his actions, or of her own jumbled up feelings in response. She wanted to focus on something else for a while, on a problem she could actually solve, so she welcomed sleep and the transition into Aurora's Dreamworld.

~

As PLANNED, they were going in search of Princess Aurora. Sienna asked everyone to pair up so that no one would be left alone wandering the castle. It was still too new and too unfamiliar to them to feel safe wandering around it alone. To Sienna's dismay, Princess Eva latched on to her as the buddy for searching the castle.

"So," Eva began as they started their search. "Can you enlighten me as to why there are rumors flying all over court that my brother Sebastian has been holding you captive for months?"

Sienna winced.

"I went to Sebastian to ask him to train me when Papa betrothed me to Axel Forrester rather than teach me to defend myself as I asked him to. After what we went through, I never wanted to be that vulnerable again. But it was a mistake."

"Learning to defend yourself or asking Sebastian to teach you?"

"All of it!"

Eva said nothing and let the silence stretch. Eventually, Sienna gave in and continued.

"I left home for boarding school as usual, but unbeknownst to my family, I went to Port Royale instead. I didn't tell Sebastian who I was because I knew he would refuse to train me if he knew. He almost refused anyway! But without the barrier of protocol between us, I thought we actually got on well. But whatever friendship had developed between us was obliterated by our parting. He hates me now. I don't think he will ever forgive me for deceiving him, and I'm not sure I can forgive him for abandoning me when I needed his support.

"Listen to me!" she laughed hollowly. "'I needed his support.' It seems all my months of training were for nothing. As soon as I am faced with a confrontation I look to someone else to support me. Maybe Papa and Axel are right, maybe it was foolish of me to think I could protect myself."

"Don't say that, Sienna," Eva said upset. "You –"

"Sienna, we found her!" Katrina shouted running up to them, Natashya close on her heels. "You're not going to believe this – she's asleep!"

"Asleep in the Dreamworld?" Eva asked, shocked.

"Let's call the others," Sienna said, glad of the interruption to her conversation with Eva. "Then we can all go to see Aurora together and find out what's going on."

It took a while to find everyone, but once they had regrouped Katrina led them to a bedroom in the East Wing where they indeed found Aurora asleep in the canopy bed. Rosebud looked around the room unnerved.

"It's just like her room at home. It's like someone wanted her to feel comfortable here," she said. She sat down on the bed and took her sister's hand in hers. "Please wake up Aura, I need my sister back," she whispered.

"Dawn is coming," Izabella warned. They all looked toward Sienna for guidance. She didn't know what to do, but she couldn't disappoint them by admitting it. She decided to play for time. "We'll meet back in the ballroom tomorrow night as usual. Once we're all in Dreamworld, we can come back up here to check on Aurora and find out why she is asleep in Dreamworld, and how she called us here if she is." She looked around and got nods and calls of agreement in return, before the sun rose and they all faded away.

19

Princess Eva woke up as soon as the Dreamworld faded and couldn't get back to sleep. Her mind was too full of all she had learned about Sebastian and Sienna. She rose early, filled with determination. She almost laughed when Philippe tried and failed to be subtle about suggesting she pay Sebastian a visit during breakfast. She feigned obliviousness initially with a wink to Marianne who did her best to hide her own laughter. Eventually, Eva relented and told Philippe that she was planning on leaving for Port Royale as soon as breakfast was finished. He huffed and grumbled at her teasing, but she could see he was relieved she was going.

Her carriage pulled up outside Sebastian's castle shortly after midday. With only a brief hello to Butler, she went straight to the training room where she was sure she would find Sir Marcus. He was in the middle of one of those complicated discipline exercises that he and Sebastian favored and she had always thought looked like dancing with swords. She admired his form as he finished the routine, not wanting to break his concentration while he was spinning swords in the air like that. She gave a gentle rap on the door when he was done to announce herself.

"Princess Eva!" Marcus exclaimed, turning around in surprise and bowing to her.

"Hi Marcus," she replied, embracing him as the long-time family friend he was. "How is he doing?"

"Not great. He says he is fine, but..."

"I know. That's why I'm here. Shall we get lunch together, and you can fill me in?"

"That would be lovely. Just let me freshen up first."

Eva left him to get changed and headed to the parlor to wait for him. She walked past the corridor for Sebastian's study on her way, but she turned away from it and continued on. "Not ready for that confrontation yet," she muttered under her breath. She rang the bell to request lunch for two from Mrs. Chambers, and Marcus joined her just as it was being served.

He filled her in on the disastrous events of the previous morning. Most of it she had already heard from Philippe, but it was good to get a new perspective on it, especially as Marcus could also comment on the interactions between Sebastian and Sienna prior to the revelations. While she was pleased to hear how compatible her friend and her brother seemed to be, she was dismayed also that Sebastian's bruised ego might have sabotaged a genuine chance at happiness for him. With lunch finished and armed with all the information she could possibly need, Eva knew she couldn't put it off any longer.

"Is he in his study?"

"Yes. He's working on a 'new project' and he's shut himself in there since yesterday morning."

"Wish me luck." Eva gathered her resolve and marched into her brother's study.

~

"EVA, JUST WHO I NEEDED," Sebastian said as she entered his study. "Here, take this sword." He held out a long sword similar to his own to her. She took it gingerly and almost dropped it when the weight surprised her. Seeing this, Sebastian snatched it back and handed her another blade, thinner and lighter, like a fencing foil. He made notes on the pages strewn across his desk while his sister stood watching him in bewilderment.

"Sebastian, *what* are you doing?" Eva demanded when it became clear that he wasn't going to stop to greet her properly.

"Hmm? Oh, I'm seeing what weapons are a suitable size for ladies to carry. I have to rethink everything I have learned to adjust it for women – they can't just do the same as men, you know. But if I am going to start recruiting women into the Rangers, I need to have appropriate training protocols for them. I'm thinking of writing a treatise with all my observations. My working title is *The Female Fighter*; what do you think?"

"You already have a female Ranger."

"Had," Sebastian corrected. "But just because the first attempt was a failure, doesn't mean the idea has no merit. I just have to select candidates more judiciously in the future."

His words felt like a slap in the face. "Is that how you think of Sienna, a failure?"

"Deceit has no place in the Rangers."

"And would you have accepted her for training if you had known she was a foreign princess?"

"No, of course not."

"Then don't you think she had a good reason for withholding her identity?"

Sebastian was sullenly silent.

"What are you really angry about, Sebastian? That Sienna hid her identity, or that she was able to?" Sebastian clenched his jaw and Eva's eyes widened. "Oh my gosh, that's it, isn't it? Your pride is hurt because you didn't realize who she really is! Instead of praising her for a successful infiltration, you're blaming her for your failure to discern the truth! She doesn't deserve to be a scapegoat for your sulking. She deserves better than that."

"Female solidarity is all well and good Eva, but this is ridiculous. 'Poor Sienna.' 'She deserves better.' *I* deserve better! She came into my home under false pretenses. Who knows what mischief she was planning?"

"She's not like that Sebastian. She just wanted to learn to defend herself. Your aspersions on her character are unbecoming."

"You don't even know her."

"Yes, I do!" Eva's voice was rising with her temper.

"I'm not talking about afternoon tea at Lady So-and-so's garden party two years ago," he said dismissively.

"Neither am I!" Eva shouted at him. "She saved my sanity and my life!" She glared at her brother in the charged silence that followed her outburst, and he stared back.

"What are you talking about?" he asked slowly.

Eva looked away. She didn't want to talk about this, didn't want to remember. But she *had* brought it up. And Sebastian needed to know if she ever wanted him to see Sienna clearly. Eva took a deep breath, and let go of the secrecy.

"Do you remember when I got sick four years ago? I was tired all the time, but sleep made me worse, not better? I couldn't tell you at the time but..."

"But you were abducted in your dreams," Sebastian concluded.

Eva was taken aback. *How did he...?* "Sienna told you?"

"Some of it."

"I knew she trusted you but I hadn't realized... We don't talk about it. None of us talk about it, *ever*. *I* haven't even told you, and you're my *brother*."

"How many of you were affected?"

"Thirteen in total. Twelve princesses –from all across Fable – and a conduit to power the spell. The Piper started at midnight. Once you heard his music, he owned you. Your will was sucked away until all that was left was *his* will, his commands. And he commanded us to dance." Her voice hitched. She swallowed hard to clear the dryness in her throat so she could continue. "It didn't matter if exhaustion overtook us, if our feet were crippled with blisters, that three-year-old Bianca was in tears. He told us to dance and we had to obey. We danced all night without rest. And when the music stopped at dawn and the Piper released his hold on us, we fell to the floor sobbing, only to wake up surrounded by families who didn't understand – who blamed us, in some cases – knowing that the following night we would have to endure it all again. There was no one to help us, no way to escape." Sebastian looked stricken with regret. Yes, he was part of the family that hadn't understood, but this wasn't about that. This was about Sienna. She plowed on, unwilling to let him derail the conversation with the wrong apologies.

"Izabella and I were the eldest of the princesses. We should have done something, but we were so lost ourselves. The best we could do was offer paltry comfort to the younger girls. But not Sienna. She refused to accept our fate." His scowl showed he was unwilling to hear about her, but Eva wouldn't let him escape that easily.

"She was only *thirteen*, Sebastian, she was just a child herself, and yet she stepped up when no one else would, to be the leader we needed. She found a way to break the Piper's hold, but she wouldn't leave without the rest of us. And when Bianca slipped up and inadvertently revealed that she was no longer under the Piper's control, Sienna volunteered to take Bianca's punishment herself to spare the child and to distract the Piper long enough for us all to escape." She saw that sink in and pressed her advantage. "I don't know what she endured after that, when the Piper discovered we were gone and she was the only princess he had left, but knowing him it was brutal. And yet she still managed to defeat him, because the dreams stopped. I don't know what it cost her.

"So you see, I don't care what wrong you think Princess Sienna has done you; I won't hear a word against her, ever. She is the strongest, bravest woman I have ever known, and for you to have made her feel less than that, to have scorned her and made her feel unworthy... I am ashamed of you, Sebastian." He started at her words, but she didn't retract them. She meant it. She wanted to throttle him for his pig-headed arrogance. "I have admired and looked up to you all my life but I look at you now and I don't even recognize you. Your ridiculous pride has blinded you to the truth. You wanted to find a woman who could be your partner rather than just your wife, and yet when she was standing right in front of you, you didn't even see her. I would have thought you of all people would understand that outward appearance does not define a person's worth. That *what* you are is not the same as *who* you are." Eva blinked back tears and heaved a deep breath, her tirade winding down. The usually articulate Sebastian was, for once, speechless. She handed the fencing foil back to him.

"I would wish you luck in your search for female Rangers," she told him quietly. "But as you have just let the best woman I know walk out of your life, I'm not sure your judgment is up to the task." She left the room quickly, so he would not have time to think of a rejoinder and she could keep the last word.

~

ALONE IN THE SILENCE, Sebastian contemplated the verbal attack from his favorite sibling. *Was it true?* he wondered. *Could I have misjudged Sienna?*

He knew he had trust issues where women were concerned. Though after what Lacey put him through it was hardly surprising. That line of thinking inevitably led to a comparison between the two women he had wanted to marry. Lacey had always been open about her family; her dishonesty was in her actions. What she said and did in front of him and behind his back were not the same, and he was so infatuated with her that he didn't see it until it was too late. Only when she ran from him and betrayed everything they had said to each other did the scales fall from his eyes and he saw her true colors at last. In many ways Camilla was similar. On paper, she was perfect and initially seemed so charming. But that charm evaporated quickly when she thought she had him hooked and decided to dictate terms.

So how did Sienna's deception measure up against those vipers? She had certainly lied about her identity. By omission or by direct words didn't matter; she had deliberately misled him about her family and status, and caused a major diplomatic incident in the process! Protocols existed for a reason and she burned them all!

But maybe she hadn't lied about her purpose in Port Royale? He had been attributing all manner of dark motives to her action, from her ingratiating knowledge of his books to her stated desire to be trained by him. But Eva had confirmed the history that Sienna had shared with him, and if that was true perhaps the rest was too? But why hide who she was? Why leave him to be blindsided in front of that cocky upstart Forrester, who thought knowing how to use a sword elevated him to equality with royalty? His hands clenched into fists as he recalled the supercilious sneer on Forrester's face as he insinuated it was Sebastian's incompetence that had allowed the Princess of Orella to live undetected in his home for so many months. He wasn't incompetent, dammit! He just hadn't been expecting the Princess of Orella to turn up unannounced at his home, nor had he expected her to be so... so...

His thoughts trailed off. Unbidden, her words from that day in the music room came back to him. *I have been overlooked and underestimated my whole life. People think they know who I am without ever actually getting to know* me. Wasn't he guilty of making the same assumptions about the Princess of Orella based on nothing but her title? Perhaps Sienna had been wise to conceal that from him if he was that prejudiced. He rummaged in his desk drawer and pulled out the discarded pile of candidates that he had selected Camilla from. He flicked through until he found what he was looking for; the profile for the youngest Orellan Princess that he had dismissed without even looking at it. He looked at it now. Under the heading 'Princess Sienna of Orella' was a portrait. Even in the formal pose, he could see the mischievous glint in her eye, the suggestion that at any moment she could jump up and run off, too exuberant a personality to ever be pinned down. He missed her smile.

He couldn't get the stricken look on her face as he turned away from her out of his mind. What he would give to go back and erase that moment! He should have punched that supercilious smirk right off Forrester's face rather than let that soldier take Sienna from his home. A princess didn't belong with a *soldier*. How stupid his concerns about her acceptability to Philippe and the court seemed now. She was every bit his match socially. A foreign princess, who could bring the alliances and trading that Orella could, outshone every Vitalian noblewoman.

Sienna outshone *every* woman, and he let her go.

What had he done?

~

Eleven princesses hurried up the staircase to Aurora's room. They all made suggestions about how to wake her – shouting loudly, shaking her, cold water, even pricking her finger with a needle (despite Rosebud's objections) – but none of their attempts worked. Aurora slept on.

"It's the curse," Princess Rosebud said dejectedly, slumping to the ground. "Even in the Dreamworld, she's caught in its snare."

"All curses can be broken," Selena said. "You can't cast a spell without an 'undo' clause, even if that clause is designed to be nearly impossible to invoke." No one doubted her; of all of them, Selena had had the greatest exposure to magic.

"So, we find out what the clause was and we can break the curse?" Izabelle clarified. Selena nodded.

"Rose, you said that your parents had a plan to break the curse," Natashya remembered. "So do they know what the clause was? Do *you* know?"

"True love's kiss," Rose spat in disgust. "My parents couldn't accept that finding true love by sixteen was an impossible goal, especially for a royal. They were certain that if Aurora met enough men that one of them was sure to be or become her true love, and then they would have a curse-breaker on hand and the curse would all be over in a few hours. But they were too proud to admit that the lofty Northavens could have been cursed. So they paraded Aura around and offered her to anyone who showed interest, without saying why. She hated it."

"That's what the 'Desperate Debutante' was about?" Eva asked, appalled. "Poor Aurora!"

"I don't suppose she's interested in girls, is she?" Valentina asked Rosebud.

"No! She just never found a man she could respect, never mind like. Hardly surprising when you consider they were in their twenties or older and she was thirteen."

"Well then," Valentina drawled looking pointedly around the room. "Knowing the clause doesn't help us because none of us is her type." The girls looked at each other and realized that she was right. The hopeful energy that had buoyed them up a moment before drained away.

"Now what?" Izabella asked, stifling a yawn. Instinctively, they looked to Sienna, expecting that she would have answers.

"Oh!" she exclaimed. "I've just realized something. Aurora is asleep!"

They stared at her.

"Really, Si?" Natashya drawled. "You've just realized that now?"

"No, I mean, she's asleep *in Dreamworld*. When we were with the Piper, his music stopped us from sleeping, so we were always exhausted when we woke from the Dreamworld. But there is no Piper here to stop us now, and Aurora is asleep. That means we can all sleep too, so we won't make ourselves ill with fatigue again while we try to solve this."

Tired smiles broke out as they realized she was right. They wandered off to explore the rest of the East Wing and select bedrooms for each of them from the many on offer. Izabelle and Selena guided Rosebud out, conscious that she would not get the rest she needed if she stayed by her sister's bedside. When everyone had left, Sienna slumped in a chair, glad to drop the pretense.

"Are you okay?"

Eva was standing in the doorway. Sienna hadn't even realized she was there. She didn't bother trying to muster false cheerfulness; Eva had already seen her façade collapse.

"I'm not sure I remember what 'okay' feels like. Everyone is expecting me to have answers and I don't even know what the questions are. I was fooling myself, thinking that we could defeat this curse alone. Just like I was fooling myself thinking I could be a Red Hood. I need to start being realistic in my aspirations. Maybe I can make being a good wife my goal."

"What do you mean?"

"Papa was so furious about me running away and so worried about what could have happened to me, that he has already set a date for the wedding in my absence. Axel informed me of it today. He and I will be married tomorrow week."

"But Sienna, you don't even like him!"

"Maybe I just didn't give him a chance," Sienna suggested. Even to her own ears she sounded more resigned than hopeful.

"He is a good man," she continued in the same flat tone. "I'm sure we can find some common ground. And he can protect me and keep me safe, which is all I've ever wanted, really. Perhaps, this has all worked out for the best." She saw Eva open her mouth to retort, but she didn't want to discuss this anymore. It was done. She said goodnight and hurried from Aurora's room to find a bedroom of her own where she could be alone with her regrets.

TEARS SPRANG to Eva's eyes as she watched her friend leave.

"Oh Sienna," she whispered to the silent room. "What did my stupid brother do to you to break your spirit so?"

20

"I'm going to marry Sienna!"

Eva and Marcus looked up from their breakfast at the pronouncement from a much more cheerful Sebastian.

"Well that might be difficult," Eva retorted coolly, "Seeing as bigamy is illegal in both Vitalia and Orella."

"What are you talking about?" A hint of alarm colored Sebastian's tone.

"I'm talking about her fiancé, or had you forgotten that detail? They've set a date. Princess Sienna of Orella will wed Lord Axel Forrester within a seven-night."

"No! Why would she agree to that? She despises Forrester."

"Because she needs to feel safe. And you threw her out of the one place she felt safest and destroyed her belief in her ability to protect herself at the same time, so she is settling for the only safety left."

"But she is so much better than Forrester. Why would she think she needs his protection? She could wipe the floor with him."

"Yes, I remember you saying that exact thing to her as you kicked her out," Marcus said sarcastically.

"I've lost her," Sebastian whispered hoarsely as he sank into a seat. "I've lost the only woman I could truly love."

"Do you mean that?" Eva rounded on him. "Do you really love her? The real Sienna and not some idolized fantasy of her?"

"Yes."

"Then *fight* for her, you dolt! She's not married yet."

"She doesn't want me."

"How do you know? Did you ever ask *her*?"

"I don't need to. She is young, beautiful and a princess to boot. I am a crippled old man. All I have to offer a woman is a title, and she already has one of her own."

"Oh, get over yourself. Those are your hang-ups, not hers! There is only one way that you will know whether she would ever return your love and that's to *ask* her. She may turn you down, but if you truly love her then that is a risk worth taking. Fight for her, rather than regretting forever letting pride hold you back."

Sebastian stood up, a new light shining in his eyes. "I need to talk to Philippe." He hurried to his study to fetch the magic mirror to call his brother.

"Mirror, mirror, in my hand, Show me the strongest in the land."

"Morning Sebastian, I was going to call you shortly, actually. I've spoken with the Duke of Bergamy and arranged for him and his sister Yvette to come to visit you."

"Cancel it."

"I beg your pardon?"

"Cancel it, Philippe. There is no point sending any more eligible ladies to visit me because I have already found the only woman I want to marry."

"When did this happen?"

"Months ago: the only woman in the world that I will marry is Princess Sienna of Orella. If she'll have me, of course."

"And if she won't?"

"Then I won't marry at all."

"But what about me? What about Marianne?"

"I'm sorry Philippe, I know you wanted me to marry to give you an heir, but Sienna is my Marianne. If she does refuse me, I won't insult the memory of what might have been by marrying a poor man's imitation of her. You and Marianne need to find another strategy – adopt, wish upon a star, make a deal with the fae – but I need to follow my own path, and that path is leading me to Orella."

"Well, I wish you luck. Just think of the trade alliance with Orella if you can win her over! The fact she would make you happy is just a bonus."

"She makes me more than happy, Philippe. She makes me whole."

"Then what are you still talking to me for? Go get her, Sebastian!"

WITHIN THE HOUR he had packed a small case with the bare essentials. He was traveling light, to make better time riding for the capital once his ship docked in Orella. He was hoping that going by sea would mean he could make up some of the lost time between him and Forrester. Orella had the fastest ships in Fable, so he was already at a disadvantage. Marcus and Eva waited at the doorway to see him off.

"Here," said Eva, handing Sebastian the enchanted hand mirror. "Take this with you so you can keep in contact with me. And I am in contact with Sienna each night, so I can keep you updated. Is there anything you want me to tell her?"

"Everything I want to say I owe it to her to say in person. But there is something she needs to know. Can you tell her that she is the Winter Siege? She'll know what it means."

"Um, sure," Eva agreed, baffled. She waved as he spurred his horse and galloped out of the courtyard, the four Rangers who were escorting him to the port keeping pace with him.

"Do you think he'll make it to Orella in time?" Marcus asked once they had disappeared from view.

"I hope so," Eva said with a sigh. "But from the way Sienna spoke about him the other night, I'm afraid he might already be too late."

SIENNA STOOD at the prow of the ship, her face turned into the salty spray. In just seven days she would be married to Lord Axel Forrester. The noose of inevitability was tightening around her, but she was too disheartened and indifferent to object. She stared into the blue waters racing past below her. There were merfolk in this stretch of the sea, though she couldn't see any at the moment. Did mermaids learn to fight if they wanted to? she wondered. Did their fathers listen to them, and not force them to marry pompous twats? Probably. Life would definitely be simpler under the sea. Lost in her musings, she did not notice she had company until she turned around and found Lord Forrester standing beside the most senior of the ladies-in-waiting, Contessa di Silva. Sienna didn't care enough to inquire about the whereabouts of the other two ladies. She nodded to Forrester to acknowledge him, but couldn't muster the enthusiasm for a more verbose welcome. Undeterred, Forrester stepped up to stand beside her and attempted to engage her in conversation. The Contessa stepped back so she could chaperone without eaves-dropping.

"It is good to see you out of your cabin, Princess Sienna," he began. "When you didn't join us at all yesterday, I was worried that you might be ill." He paused, perhaps hoping for some further acknowledgment, but Sienna continued to stare out to sea dully. When it became clear she was not going to respond he sighed and slouched against the rail beside her. That *did* get a reaction. Sienna looked at him askance, as if to chide him on his lack of decorum. He lifted one shoulder in a half-shrug and smiled ruefully at her.

"We have never had much chance to get to know each other, you and I, have we Princess? You spent so much of your time at school and we were always surrounded by others when you came home for the holidays. I probably haven't shown you my best self either, in the times we were together. It is hard to be yourself when you feel the weight of expectations pressing in on you from all sides.

"The greatest pressure comes from the expectation I set for myself: to ensure your safety and in doing so to prove myself worthy of you. Such a simple aim in theory. But in practice, so difficult. Sometimes the only way to protect something wild is to tame it first. You have always had a spark of wildfire in you, a fearlessness that blinds you to the potential dangers that surround you. Keeping you safe from yourself in your own home was an almost impossible task. I have been so worried these past few weeks, wondering if you were well, scared of the peril you could have gotten yourself into, hating that I wasn't there to protect you. I dreaded to think what harm could have befallen you if unscrupulous people took advantage of your trusting nature."

"Worried what my father would say if you failed in the duty he set you, you mean."

Axel stared at her in surprise, surprised she said anything at all as much as by what she said. He weighed her words. Though she had spoken disinterestedly, he concluded that she believed what she said of his motives and that it bothered her, no matter how much she pretended it didn't.

"No one coerced me into being your protector or your fiancé, Princess," he told her softly. He hesitated, wondering how best to explain it. "I remember the first time I saw you. I had just been promoted to officer status and Commander Hawthorne was giving me the tour of the palace. You were maybe ten years old and your governess was trying to teach you the proper composition for flower arrangments when we passed your classroom. You kept insisting that the wildflowers you had picked yourself deserved to be featured beside the prize-winning roses from the Queen's garden because 'just because they grew in different soil, doesn't make them less pretty.'

"I had been feeling overwhelmed and out of place among the aristocracy who make up the officer ranks, and your words struck a chord with me. I felt a connection to you from that moment that is absent with the rest of your family. You have a way of brightening a room just by entering it, and I missed your presence when you returned to school each year. I could hardly ask to woo you when you were still a child, but as soon as you turned sixteen I asked your father for permission to court you, not really expecting him to agree. Imagine my surprise when he offered me your hand instead!

"I know I am not your choice for a husband, but if you give me the chance I will slay any dragon for you Princess, and be your shield from all the world's harms. It will be my honor to cherish you and keep you safe all the days of our lives."

SHE TURNED BACK to face him and this time actually *looked* at him. His skin was bronzed from his time outdoors with the army. He was tall - a full head taller than her. That height difference used to bother her, but having been around the Rangers for the past few months, Sienna was acclimatized to being the shortest in the room. The tailored jacket of a nobleman could not hide the definition of his muscles underneath, arms strengthened by years of swinging a sword in honor of her father and in defense of her kingdom. Though his clothes were perfectly tailored to his frame, he still looked uncomfortable in them. Armour was obviously his preferred attire. His eyes were a little small for his face, perhaps, and his mouth too wide, but there was a gentleness to him that she had not seen before. Or maybe it had always been there and she had just been too self-absorbed to notice.

"Sienna."

He stared at her. "I beg your pardon?"

"You are going to be my husband. You might as well call me by my given name."

He bowed in acknowledgment. "Good day... Sienna."

She looked back out across the sea again as he walked away, but she no longer saw it. The last half-hour had been full of revelations she had not expected. She pursed her lips in an unhappy line as she absorbed them all.

Could she have misjudged Axel as badly as she had misjudged Sebastian?

The mood was somber in the Dream Castle that night. Sienna went straight to her bedroom. She was morose about her own situation and because of her failure to do anything useful to help Aurora, and she just wanted to avoid everyone. She especially wanted to avoid Eva; Sienna didn't think she could face hearing about Sebastian while she wallowed in her current self-pity.

A knock on the door made her bury her head deeper under the blankets. *I should have locked the door*, she grumbled to herself as she heard footsteps entering the room even though she hadn't answered.

"Sienna? Are you awake?" The voice wasn't Eva's; Sienna recognized the cadence of Princess Natashya's accent. She decided that she was not in so bad a place that she was hiding from her best friend, and reluctantly drew the covers down and sat up in the bed. Natashya took one look at her, then climbed onto the bed beside her and pulled her into a bear hug. She didn't say anything, just offered her silent support, and it was enough. Eventually Sienna drew back, surreptitiously wiping away a tear. It felt so good to have a friend, a shoulder to cry on – literally and figuratively.

"So, what's up Asha?" she asked putting her self-pity aside and focusing on her friend. Natashya had sought her out for a reason.

"It's Odette. I'm really concerned that she still hasn't appeared. It's been a week since Aurora brought us here. No one can stay awake that long, but I don't know why else she would be excluded from the spell. I'm worried something might be really wrong."

"You're right," Sienna said. "We've all been focusing on Aurora but there is another Princess who may need our help. Though I'm not sure what we can do for her either," she concluded dejectedly.

. . .

NATASHYA'S HEART sank at Sienna's defeated tone. She had been hoping that Sienna would have some great insight to help her, but she could see that Sienna was barely holding herself together.

"I am planning to pay a visit to Bretonnia," Natashya confided. "Odette is approaching her majority so her coronation will be soon. As the future Queen of Siverus, I would be a good choice to represent our family at the Coronation."

"That's a brilliant idea!" Sienna exclaimed. The momentary animation gave Natashya hope that her friend's spirit had not been completely extinguished. "The coronation provides the perfect motivation to travel cross-continent, without having to reveal your suspicions or concerns. When are you thinking of going?"

"As soon as possible. Tomorrow, hopefully. I wrote to Odette as soon as we realized she wasn't in Dreamworld proposing the visit, and I got a reply yesterday. I think it was written by an aide rather than by Odette herself, it's all formal and stiff. Who would dare interfere with the future Queen's private correspondence with another royal? Something is definitely wrong but at least the letter says that Odette will receive me on our arrival in Bretonnia, so I will have a chance to ask her myself."

"Our?"

"I'm bringing Alexei with me," Natashya explained, with an indulgent sigh for her rogueish twin. "He's bored at home and liked Odette when she came to stay with us three years ago, so I think a trip to Bretonnia might be just the thing to rouse him out of his current lethargy."

"How is Alexei? I haven't seen him in ages."

"Bored, as I said, now that Lord Russia has gone back to his father's estate and isn't available to accompany him hunting and carousing any more. I finally convinced him to stop moping long enough to pack a trunk tonight. Alexei needs a focus. Or perhaps a wife."

"I pity the girl!"

"I wish Alexei would marry *you* Sienna. Then we could be sisters for real."

Sienna started to laugh, her first genuine laugh since Forrester had arrived at Port Royale. "Asha, I love you, but not enough to shackle myself to your twin brother for the rest of our lives! You know we'd make a horrible couple."

"I know, I know."

"We could still be sisters though if you marry *my* brother."

"Ew, Luca is only fifteen! He's much too young for me!"

"It's not that big an age gap," Sienna sighed. Asha could see from the distant look in her eyes that Sienna was no longer talking about her younger brother, so she didn't carry the joke further by protesting.

"We'll both find our proper Princes one day. We just may have to kiss a lot of frogs in the meantime," she said instead.

"My frog kissing days are over; this time next week I'll be married," Sienna stated. "And I haven't even gotten to kiss any frogs – or princes," she added wistfully.

Asha didn't know what to say to that. She knew the pressure Sienna's parents were putting on her to get married, and she could see that Sienna no longer had the will to fight them on it. She was pleased her own parents were more supportive and respected her independence because she wasn't ready to give it up yet – and she was older than Sienna! So Asha did the only thing she could for her friend and hugged her again to remind her she was not alone.

21

The fanfare that accompanied Sienna's return to the capital city Trefiumi was nauseating. Normally, she loved the view of the harbor filled with ships from all over the world, but today she barely saw them. The travelers alighted onto the dock and boarded the carriages waiting for them. Sienna looked out the window to avoid talking to her companions. The white-painted houses flashed by outside. The bougainvillea draped over trellises between the buildings, adding splashes of color and the familiar scent of her childhood. She focused on the rhythmic noise of the carriage wheels across the cobblestones, trying to drown out her other thoughts and misery.

The road turned and Sienna saw her home, gleaming in the Orellan sunlight. Built at the confluence of the three rivers the city was named for, Palazzo di Trefiumi seemed to rise out of the water itself. Like the other buildings in the city, the Palazzo was white, but it achieved its coloring because of the stone used in its construction, rather than via painting. The domed roof was covered in blue glass, making it sparkle.

As the carriage pulled up at the palace entrance, Sienna

was dismayed to see staff and minor nobility arrayed on the steps to welcome them. Forester smiled graciously at all of them, basking in the attention. Sienna gritted her teeth but followed his lead. It was her home, for pity's sake, no one needed to welcome her to it. She wished she could just go to her room and have some space to tend her emotional wounds in peace. But it seemed that was not in the cards.

Forrester continued through the palace to the formal receiving room, where both her parents awaited them. Queen Carmen was waif-thin and played on her delicate appearance. She acted nervy and distressed to get her own way. Her dark hair was pinned to her head in the severe style she favored. Carmen thought it made her look regal. Sienna thought it made her look judgemental and haughty – though that might be just because she knew those traits first hand. Her mother embraced her, simultaneously sobbing in relief and chiding her for the worry she had caused. Sienna squirmed guiltily, despite knowing her mother's manipulative ways.

King Stefano was jovial where his wife was condescending. He commended Forrester on successfully locating and returning Sienna. At the King's urging, Forrester launched into a detailed (and to Sienna's mind, embellished) account of how he found and rescued her. When he got to the part about where she had been for the past several months, Queen Carmen interjected.

"You mean to tell me that the Vitalian prince has been holding our baby girl all this time? This indignity will not stand! We should launch trade sanctions against Vitalia immediately!"

"No." Sienna had let Axel tell his story his way without interrupting, but she would not budge on this point.

"Why not, Carissa?" her father asked.

"Because Prince Sebastian didn't kidnap me; I imposed

myself on him. And he was nothing but a gentleman throughout my time in Port Royale. It is not fair to penalize an entire country for my choices."

"But why would you go there?"

"Because I wanted to learn to fight, to protect myself, and you wouldn't let me learn here."

"There is no need for that, Princess Sienna," Forrester said earnestly. "I am here to protect you."

"And a good thing too," Stefano agreed. Sienna had never doubted her father's love for her, or his good intentions. But he was too set in his ways. As far as he was concerned, Sienna was still a helpless little girl looking for safety. They were locked in the time of her captivity when he became so fearful for her that his protectiveness kicked into overdrive. He never noticed that she grew up, or that her needs changed. "I'm so pleased the date for your wedding is finally set. We've been working hard here to get everything set up. Though of course, your mother has been planning the event for so long that it's mostly done already!"

"I had several outfits made for you," the Queen told Sienna. As the 'beauty,' Sienna was Carmen's prized jewel amongst her daughters, a pretty doll to be played with. "But they are based on your measurements from before you left for Cadia, so you'll need to try them so the seamstresses can make the final adjustments. Why don't we do that now? Then we can meet up with the boys later for dinner. You will dine with us Axel, won't you?"

"It would be my pleasure, Your Majesty."

The Queen sailed out of the room, with Sienna reluctantly trailing in her wake.

Several hours later, Sienna had lost count of how many gowns she had tried on. She stood in her assigned spot and let the seamstresses do their thing while the Queen and her ladies-in-waiting admired or critiqued each one.

Sienna stared out the window at the horizon and let her mind wander to more important things. How was she going to help Aurora? Her sleep curse was so deep, she was even asleep *within her dreams*. No one knew where she was, and the League seeing her in their dreams wasn't much good when they couldn't communicate with her to learn where her physical body was.

"Sienna, are you even listening to me?" Belatedly, Sienna registered that her mother had been talking to her.

"Really, what's the point in me ordering dresses in your favorite colors and styles if you won't even pause long enough to admire and appreciate them?" the Queen continued petulantly.

"That's it!" Sienna gasped. "Mama, thank you."

"For what?" the Queen asked, perplexed. But Sienna was already gone. The idea was nascent, but she was sure she was on the right track. Now she just had to wait for nightfall so she could get back to Aurora and confirm it.

"ROSEBUD! ROSEBUD!" Sienna shouted for the other princess as she raced through the dream castle that night. Princess Natashya looked out of one of the rooms as she ran past, startled by the commotion.

"She's in Aurora's room," Natashya told Sienna, falling into step behind her. "What's the matter?"

"I think I've solved part of the mystery about Aurora's curse, but I need to check something with Rose first."

Princess Rosebud looked up as the two girls burst into the room. There were dark circles under her eyes; she had not tried to get sleep while in the Dreamworld as the other Princesses had, but remained at her sister's side hoping for some sign of awareness from her.

"Rose, you said that this room is like Aurora's room in Northaven," Sienna began. "This is important, so I need you to be sure: are there definite items unique to Aurora here, or is it just generically similar to her own room?"

Rosebud blinked and tried to focus on the room around her rather than its occupant. "Um, there are three really flat pillows under Aura's head rather than one full one, which was something she always insisted on at home no matter how often I pointed out the two options were the same height. And there are multiple light covers on the bed too, instead of one heavy blanket. And that chessboard," Rosebud added, pointing to the corner of the room. "Aura loves chess. When she started to show proficiency in it, Father commissioned a special set for her. Rather than standard black and white, it is green and gold like the Northaven flag – and that board is just the same!"

"So it's no coincidence then," Sienna said, her eyes gleaming with delight. "Someone went to a lot of trouble to surround Aurora with familiar and cherished things."

"So?" Rosebud asked. She had already said this the night they found the room. She couldn't see why Sienna was getting so excited about it now.

"Why would you go to the trouble of creating a familiar environment for someone who will never be awake to see it?"

"You wouldn't," Natashya answered promptly. Her eyes widened as the implication sank in. "Which means... Aurora must be 'awake' within the Dreamworld at some point to warrant the effort that whoever took her has put into this place."

"Exactly!"

"You think Aura isn't fully lost in her curse?" Rose asked, scarcely daring to hope it was true.

"I think she is still under a sleeping spell," Sienna said

softly. “But I think she is more aware than we have seen her so far. My guess is that she is ‘awake’ in the Dreamworld during the daytime. But what this means is that she may be able to tell us more about her situation and may even be able to tell us where her physical location is so we can find her and bring her home.”

“That would be amazing,” Rose whispered, tears filling her eyes.

“Let’s get the others,” Natashya suggested. “Then we can all decide what message to leave for Aurora and how to deliver it.” It took a while to gather everyone and agree on what to say. Rosebud was set to write an essay on the large slate they had found in the pantry until Selena reminded them all that they didn’t know who else had access to the Dreamworld, nor what their intentions might be toward Aurora. That sobered them all, and they decided to be more circumspect in their communication, at least until they had a better idea of what was going on. The final wording said:

We gathered again for the Midnight Ball but were saddened you couldn’t join us. There is no music yet; is the piper with you? Is that why you have been detained? Do write soon, if you can, but remember Rule #24.

“There, that should do it,” Rosebud said as she finished writing. They had agreed that it would be best if Rose wrote the message so that her sister would recognize the handwriting and thus have an extra clue to decipher their meaning. Rule #24 was Rose’s addition, a reference to Frau Heinkle who had been their governess for many years and was full of rules for proper princess behavior. Rule #24 said that “A Princess should always guard her correspondence closely; you never know when an unscrupulous person may try to read it.” She just hoped Aurora remembered Frau Heinkle’s lessons.

With nothing else to be done, the princesses drifted out

of Aurora's room, Izabella again taking charge of Rosebud and leading her away. Princess Eva followed Sienna to her room. She had been watching the younger princess all night and noticed that after the initial spark that had given them the way forward, Sienna had withdrawn from the discussion, leaving it to the others to work out the next steps. It was like that moment of inspiration had taken all of her energy and she had nothing left to share with anyone. Now, Eva was alarmed by how lackluster and passive the usually vibrant Sienna appeared, when she thought she was alone.

"Sienna?" she called out, alerting Sienna to her presence.

Sienna's shoulders tensed then slumped even further. Eva wouldn't have believed it possible. "What is it, Eva?" she asked without turning around. She reached her room and walked inside, but she left the door ajar. Eva took this as a tacit invitation and followed her inside. She stood awkwardly in the doorway unsure how to react to this shadow of her savior.

"Sebastian's an idiot!" she blurted out. It wasn't how she intended to start this conversation, but she reflected that perhaps it was what needed to be said. "If it helps, he knows he's an idiot," she added. No reaction from Sienna. "He is on his way to Orella to apologize."

"He doesn't owe me an apology," Sienna said quietly. "He doesn't owe me anything."

"I disagree, I think he owes you more than he can ever repay, but that is for him to discuss with you, not me." Eva hesitated, unsure whether she should pass on her brother's message, especially when she didn't understand it. But she figured that she couldn't hurt Sebastian's case by sharing it, given the low esteem Sienna currently held him in. Who knew, it might even help.

"Sebastian asked me to give you a message. He said you

would understand. He said to tell you that you're the 'Winter Siege.' Does that make sense to you?"

The phrase resonated within Sienna. There was only one thing he could be referring to. The words appeared in her mind as clearly as if she was reading them. *There is no greater demonstration of resilience than withstanding the winter siege. It takes a depth of inner courage to look around at enemies on all sides and yet still stand strong. It takes confidence in your own strength to endure those adverse conditions and not falter. But those with the resilience of the Winter Siege within them, know that spring will thaw the snows and turn the tide.*

"Yes, it makes sense." A lump formed in her throat. Sebastian believed in her. He thought she could do it, could be more than everyone else expected of her. Her fate was her own.

"So," Eva pressed. "What does it mean?"

"It means spring is coming."

"And Sebastian is spring?"

"No," Sienna smiled, the light returning to her eyes. "I am."

22

The next night, Sienna met the others on the staircase as they all raced to Aurora's room with a single purpose. Everyone was anxious to see if she had responded and, if so, what she could tell them about her circumstances and, by extension, their own. But when they got to her room they were disappointed; everything was exactly as they had left it the previous night. Aurora was still asleep in the canopy bed and the slate still rested by the fireplace. Sienna had hoped that Aurora would have written a reply to them on it, but only the message they had composed the night before was present. It was Cordelia who spotted it first.

"Look!" she cried, pointing at the slate. The others gathered around her to see what she had spotted. At the bottom of the message they had written, there was now an arrow pointing to the right. Katrina followed the arrow to the writing desk and exclaimed in triumph when she found the letter sitting there. It was addressed to Princess Rosebud van Northaven in a flowing cursive script. Katrina passed the letter over to the other girl.

"That's Aurora's writing," Rosebud said quietly. She

swallowed the lump in her throat and opened the letter. As she read through the letter, a smile broke out across her face.

"You were right, Sienna! She is awake some of the time, or at least conscious. The sleeping curse did take effect, but her body was brought here for her safety while she is vulnerable. Listen to this:

Dear Rosa,

I can't believe my wish worked and you can contact me here! And the whole League of Princesses is here too? Thank you all for coming; I was so scared to be trapped here alone when I felt my curse start to take hold. I didn't think it had worked, as I hadn't seen any of you yet. I don't know where you found that blackboard, but it was an inspired idea to send a message to me. However, it is much too cumbersome and I have too much to say for me to use, so I'm writing a letter instead. I appreciate your warning about Rule #24, Rosa, but it's not something we need to worry about here. The Piper doesn't have me. I was brought to this castle by O – he hasn't told me his full name, because names have power. I can't tell you much about him either, but he has told me enough to convince me he means me no harm. In fact, he's like a guardian angel looking out for me.

I can't tell you where I am, because I don't know. O says he can't tell me, because if he reveals my location then the concealing spells he has woven around the castle for my protection will be broken and I will be vulnerable again. I know it must sound like I'm a prisoner – especially to Princess Izabella, given what she went through – but I'm really not. Or rather, the imprisonment comes from my curse which traps me in my mind, rather than from O who is just keeping me safe until the curse can be broken.

I don't know how to break the curse. Not yet. But tell Princess Sienna that I haven't forgotten her words from four years ago when we founded the League of Princesses. I am not waiting for some prince to save me. I'm going to find a way to save myself. I don't know how yet, but I'm hoping you and the rest of the League will help me figure it out.

Please write again! It gets so lonely here, even though O visits when he can. I never considered that I would be aware of the time passing while under this curse.

Stay safe and stay strong. Remember I love you, and no matter what else changes that never will.

Love Aura."

"Well, that's useless," Valentina griped. "Aurora doesn't know where she is, and the only person who *does* know won't tell us. We're right back to square one in terms of finding her."

"Not necessarily," Selena said slowly. "The letter says that the protections on her location are magical. Magic has rules but it also has loopholes. If this O is really her friend and not her jailor then he won't object to us exploiting those loopholes; we just have to find them. For example, he says that *he* can't reveal the location, but maybe Aurora herself can?"

"But she said she doesn't know her location."

"But she may know enough to help us work it out. What is the view from the windows in daylight? What time are sunrise and sunset? How hot or cold is it? These are all clues that may help us narrow down her location."

"Her location is the secondary concern," Sienna said, joining the conversation. "Wherever she is, she is currently protected, but I assume those concealment spells will fail the moment anyone discovers the castle?" She looked to Selena for confirmation and got a nod in reply. "So there is no point in barging in there and breaking those spells if we can't offer her protections that are at least as good as them, or break the curse outright. We don't even know why O felt Aurora needed protecting so much that he whisked her away and told no one about it. But she was cursed for a reason..."

"Hey!" Rosebud objected.

"I don't mean that she *deserved* to be cursed. But whoever cursed her picked her for a reason, picked this curse for a reason. Rose, do you know who placed the curse?"

"No. It happened at her naming ceremony, so it was before I was born. I guess my parents must know, but they refused to talk about it. As if ignoring the curse would mean it wouldn't take effect."

"Do you think O would know? And if so, would he tell Aurora?"

"He might," Selena replied. "But if he is a mage he would be bound by the Mage's Code not to interfere in another mage's spell.

"So what do you call this then?" Natashya asked, waving her arm to indicate all of their surroundings.

"A loophole. Technically, placing spells to ensure that Aurora's body is safe and undiscovered is not interfering with her succumbing to the sleeping curse."

"So, we have two main questions for Aurora: who cursed you and what clues can you give us about your current whereabouts," Natashya summarized. "Rosebud, are you happy to draft the reply?"

"Of course," Rosebud agreed eagerly.

"Then we'll leave you to it," Eva said firmly, conscious that there were probably things that Rosebud would want to put in a letter to her sister that she wouldn't necessarily want to share with the rest of them. Eva, Izabelle, and Selena herded the younger girls out and closed the door behind them. Rosebud was left alone at the writing desk, her only company her comatose sister, asleep on the bed behind her.

~

EVERY MOMENT of Sebastian's voyage to Orella was nausea-inducing. Not because he was sea-sick – in fact, he was a very good sailor – but because of his anxiety over the reception that awaited him there. He stood on the bow of the ship staring forward hoping to see Sienna's vessel on the horizon. He interrogated the crew about the speeds they were achieving, the time it was taking, and any strategies to get there sooner, until the Captain had enough and confined Sebastian to his quarters, prince or no. It was a long four days, so when land came into sight Sebastian was standing on deck again ready to go. He barely waited for the ropes to be tied to the docks in Trefiumi harbor before he leaped from the ship and hurried to the nearest stage-coach tavern. He paid double to be able to take the horse already saddled, even though it had been prepared for another customer, and rode as fast as he could toward the center of the city and the palace clearly visible there. The gold and white bunting lining every street was a stark reminder of the pending nuptials he needed to disrupt. He gritted his teeth and rode on.

A palace groom came over to take the horse from him when he dismounted in the courtyard. Sebastian took a steadying breath then strode up the palace steps and knocked on the door. A footman opened the door and looked at him with poorly disguised curiosity.

"Can I help you, sir?"

"Sebastian, Prince of Vitalia and Commander of the King's Army, to see Princess Sienna of Orella," Sebastian announced. Curiosity turned to doubt, but the footman ushered Sebastian into a salon to wait.

"I'll fetch the Maester, sir. Em. I mean Your Highness." The footman scuttled from the room in search of his boss, leaving Sebastian alone. Sebastian could understand the footman's confusion. He hardly looked very princely in his slightly crumpled traveling clothes, with the mud of the port still on his boots, but he had no thought to spare for the lackey's dilemma. His thoughts were full of Sienna. He paced agitatedly across the salon and back again. Where was that Maester? He was taking forever to get here and Sebastian had already been waiting far too long. To be so close to Sienna, in her home, and still not be able to talk to her... He grunted again in frustration and paced some more.

Finally, the Maester bustled into the salon with an apologetic frown.

"Your Highness, welcome to Orella," he said with an elaborate bow, clearly recognizing Sebastian despite his attire. "Unfortunately, we were not expecting you, so do not have a formal welcome prepared."

"Oh, it didn't occur to me to send word I was coming," Sebastian replied awkwardly, inwardly cursing his lack of planning.

"No, of course not when you were coming for the wedding, but I'm afraid you missed it."

"What do you mean?"

"The wedding of Princess Sienna and Lord Forrester is over."

"No," Sebastian croaked inaudibly. The room started to spin, or perhaps that was just his vision. His worst fear had been realized. He was too late to fight for her; Sienna was already married.

23

wo Days Earlier

YOU ARE THE WINTER SIEGE.

The phrase was foremost in Sienna's mind when she awoke. Sebastian was right. She *was* stronger than this. Time to step up and fight for what she wanted, rather than enduring in silence to appease her parents. She thought about it as she got dressed, and while sitting at breakfast with her parents, Lord Forrester, and her younger brother Luca. It seemed there was no way to ease it into the conversation gently, so she just announced it bluntly instead.

"I want to dissolve my engagement."

Silence followed her outburst. The Queen frowned. "What's brought this on? Is it pre-wedding jitters? You've been looking forward to it so."

"No, Mama. *You* have been looking forward to my wedding. *I* don't want to get married. Papa, I'm only seventeen. Violetta was twenty-two when she got married. Olivia still isn't married! Why are you in such a hurry to marry me off?"

"You know that's not what this is, Carissa. You're my little girl – I just want you to be safe. And Axel will take good care of you."

"But I'm not a little girl anymore, Papa, and I can take care of myself."

"I know you like to think so, but there are bad people in the world who could hurt you. That's why you need a protector. Isn't that right, Axel?"

Axel hastily took another mouthful of eggs to spare him answering. His cheeks were flushed, and he was clearly uncomfortable being witness to this family argument pertaining to him.

Sienna huffed in frustration. She knew her father only wanted what was best for her, but his obtuseness in listening to her thoughts on the topic was maddening. He didn't support independent thought from women; to his mind, they had neither the education nor the capacity to make important decisions without some guidance. Even though he had ensured that his daughters receive the best education, he still forgot that they had the ability to use it. "I don't need a protector, and I'll prove it to you! Axel, I challenge you to a duel."

Axel choked on his eggs.

"Carissa, there is no need for theatrics. Clearly, you cannot expect the Commander of my Guard to fight against an untrained girl?"

"No, of course not. But I'm not untrained. And the challenge has been issued now, so the Commander must accept it or be dishonored."

"I accept," Axel said in a strangled voice. Lower, so only Sienna could hear him, he added, "That was a mean trick."

"I'm sorry," she replied equally quietly, and she meant it. "It was the only way I could think of to make him see."

"I don't want to hurt you."

"You won't."

Queen Carmen was peeved. "And when is this little tantrum duel meant to occur? Might I remind you the wedding is in five days?"

"I can clear the practice ring this afternoon, Your Majesty."

"No, let's wait until tomorrow," King Stefano decided. "Hopefully my daughter will have come to her senses by then and withdraw her foolish challenge."

"Of course, Sire," Axel agreed.

Perfect little toady, Sienna thought ungraciously. She kept her own face down through the rest of the breakfast. She objected to her father's dismissive attitude, but she knew no good would come from arguing. She would make her point tomorrow on the sands of the training arena.

THE DAY of the duel dawned bright and clear. Sienna knew her father expected her to back down, but she couldn't. This was too important.

She smiled when she saw the outfit laid out for her. Her maid Emmaline was skeptical when she had told her to fetch a soldier's practice uniform from the laundry. But the treasure had come through for her, and without any of the arguments or objections Contessa di Silva would have insisted upon. Sienna briefly mourned her customized dresses left in Vitalia as she got dressed. She knew trousers would be better for this fight, even if she had access to her dresses, but she made a mental note to get replacements made as soon as possible.

She drew some curious glances as she walked through the castle to the army's training grounds, but she ignored them. The dressing rooms attached to the training grounds were communal, and she had been wondering how to navigate that with propriety, but she needn't have worried. A pageboy met her at the entrance and let her to an indoor training room that had been cordoned off for her exclusive use, on Commander Forrester's orders.

Arrayed on a bench in the room were half a dozen leather vests and multiple swords of different lengths and weights. Someone had gone to a lot of trouble to ensure she would have the right size armor and weapon entering the duel. She was quite certain it was Axel. Even though he didn't want her to fight, he was still protecting her.

She held up a few vests to gauge the size. She chose one and adjusted the belts to ensure a snug fit that wouldn't curtail her movements. Next, she assessed the blades. It reminded her of her first day in Port Royale, choosing her weapon to fight Sir Marcus. But poison or trickery wouldn't help her now. For her victory to count, she had to beat Axel in a straight fight. And she was confident that she could do it. After trying a few for weight and balance, she picked up the sword that suited her best and took a steadying breath. With Marcus, she had only been fighting for a chance; now she was fighting for her freedom. And she was going to win.

As prepared as she could be, she left her dressing room. Axel was waiting in the corridor that led to the arena. She gave him a half-smile, a rueful acknowledgment of the predicament she had put him in and a thanks for his efforts on her behalf. He just stared at her. She closed the distance between them and stood beside him.

"What?" His staring was starting to unnerve her.

"Um, your legs are visible." Crimson sneaked across his cheeks.

Sienna rolled her eyes. "Yes, I have legs, it's how I walk. Don't worry, the trousers cover them completely. Were you expecting me to fight in a dress? Come on."

Axel put his hand out to stop her. "We have to wait to be announced."

Since when? Sienna thought. *And announced to whom?* A booming voice from outside introduced them, and Axel nodded. They walked out of the dressing rooms to the bright sunshine of the arena together. Sienna's unspoken question was answered immediately. The benches on all sides of the arena were thronged.

"Why are there so many people here? I thought practice sessions were private?"

"They are, usually. But this isn't a practice session, is it? Word of your challenge spread. Everyone wants to see..."

"See you put me in my place," Sienna finished for him. Axel winced at her bald assessment but nodded.

"It's not too late to withdraw, you know?"

"I'm sorry, Axel, but it is. No one believes in me, so I have to do this to be taken seriously."

She turned to where the king and queen were sitting in the crowd and saluted them with her sword. It was a deliberate choice to eschew the courtly curtsey in favor of the soldier's salute indicating readiness. She was going to fight, and she wanted no one doubting her intentions. Axel hesitated a moment – perhaps giving her a final opportunity to back out, perhaps hoping the king would intercede and forbid the match – before raising his sword to salute the crown too.

He met her in the center of the arena, resignation, regret, and resolve flitting across his expression. She knew he wouldn't go easy on her; he just wanted to get it over with. That was okay, she didn't need easy. She held his gaze while the announcer shouted the familiar words from the sidelines.

"En garde!"

She took a deep breath and readied her stance.

"Allez!"

~

Axel opened with a swift strike, hoping to end the duel quickly. Sienna had expected him to start slowly and test her, and so had to rapidly switch tactics in response. She guessed that he saw no need to test her skills, as he had already assumed that she had none. He seemed surprised that she could respond, and she maintained her defense through all his maneuvers.

Axel was good, very good. He was one of the top five swordsmen across the entire continent of Fable, maybe even top three. But Sienna had been trained by the men ranked 1 and 2, and knew how to hold her own against them. She was a Ranger, a member of the most elite team of soldiers in Fable. She upped the tempo and switched to offense, catching Axel by surprise.

There was a subtle shift in his posture. Nothing overt, but Sienna knew how to watch her opponent for clues. He had finally recognized that there was no easy victory to be scored today and that if he wanted to secure *any* victory he would have to work for it. His head was in the game now, but it was already too late. She knew it, and he knew it; he just hadn't accepted it yet.

Sienna's heart raced and her blood thumped in her ears. And yet in that moment of heightened anticipation, she felt perfectly calm. She met him strike for strike. She could anticipate his moves and countered them almost lazily. She advanced, forcing him to give ground. This was it! She was about to prove herself in front of the whole court. The girl they had disregarded was about to trounce their celebrated paragon.

She faltered.

If she did this, Axel's reputation would be ruined. Whether they acknowledged her victory or called it a fluke, Axel would be ridiculed forever. Axel, who had organized her comfort and protection. Who was more than the overbearing critic she had thought him to be. He didn't deserve that.

If she didn't defeat him, she would have to marry him. *She* didn't deserve to be shackled to a man who, while considerate and caring, thought of her as little more than a dainty doll. But he was not any man. He represented the Orellan Army. If he was ridiculed, the Army would be as well. And if the Army was a joke, could they still be an effective deterrent to Orella's enemies? Was she jeopardizing her kingdom's security by pressing her advantage?

She could not take that risk. Her duty as a Princess and as a Ranger demanded she protect her people. But it didn't require her to give up her identity in the process. She would not destroy Axel's standing, but nor could she let him continue to dismiss her. She needed him to *know*, even if no one else would. She needed his respect.

He had capitalized on her hesitation, and only muscle memory had deflected his blows. She was paying attention now. The world narrowed to a bubble around them. Nothing else existed. She redoubled her efforts, forcing him into a defensive stance. He was tiring and she was not. She waited until she saw the realization in his eyes that he couldn't beat her. Their swords were locked together. The crowd fell silent in anticipation. Through the blades, she saw the shock register on his face before it faded into resignation. In that moment of acceptance, she reduced the pressure she was exerting and took a half-step back.

He seized the opening to take her down. He twisted the sword from her grasp, rather than draw blood. Unarmed, she conceded at once. The crowd roared and cheered for their champion. Sienna picked up her sword, shook hands with Axel, and saluted the royal box, as was customary at the end of duels. As they left the arena together, Sienna tried to not regret her choice. Axel was able to leave the arena with his dignity intact, and she had made her point.

She hadn't averted her wedding, but at least she had earned her husband's respect.

~

"You deliberately threw the fight."

Sienna looked around the corridor furtively. "Why would you say that?"

"Don't insult us both by pretending otherwise. There is no one else here." All the same, he followed her into her dressing room and closed the door to prevent them from being overheard. "I'm the Commander of the Orellan Army. I've dueled countless times, and I know when I am beaten. You could have forced me to yield, but you didn't. You were so eager to win and end our engagement before the match. Everyone was watching; no one could have denied your victory. Why did you not take your chance?"

"*Because* everyone was watching. I couldn't do that to you."

He sat down beside her. "You gave up your freedom to spare me humiliation? It's no wonder that I love you. It's okay, you don't have to say anything. I know you don't feel the same about me." He closed his eyes and took a deep breath. When he looked at her again, it was with a new resolve. "I want to call off the engagement."

"What? I thought you want to get married?"

"King Stefano told me you needed a protector. I wanted to be that person, to be the one standing between you and any harm. But you proved today that you *don't* need a protector. You don't need *me*, Sienna. And I won't be the one who cages you."

"Thank you, Axel." She kissed him on the cheek. He blushed, suddenly conscious that he was sitting with his fiancée in a dimly lit area, unchaperoned.

"Let's go tell your father," he said gruffly.

"Now?"

"No point in prolonging expectations. Leave your armor on. It makes more of an impact."

"She's out there, you know, that girl who needs you. I hope you find her soon."

"So do I," Axel agreed. But privately he wondered how anyone would ever live up to the standard set by Princess Sienna.

"GOOD, YOU'RE HERE." King Stefano ushered them into the salon. "We can get on with the wedding plans."

Queen Carmen frowned at Sienna's clothes. "Couldn't you have at least changed first?"

"No Mama, this is who I am. There isn't going to be a wedding."

"Now, now, Carissa. We humored your requests but this has gone far enough. You put on a good show, but Forester proved he is still far more capable of protecting you then leaving you to your own devices."

"Sire, I must respectfully disagree. Your daughter was

not only my equal in the arena today, she was my better. She had the opportunity to claim the match yet yielded to allow me to save face. She is more than capable of protecting herself. It is for this reason, Your Majesties, that I respectfully request you dissolve my engagement to your daughter."

"What?"

"Axel, may I have a word?" The King pulled his Commander aside. Sienna strained to listen, ignoring her mother's outraged objections. Axel was telling Stefano the same things that Sienna had been saying for months, but it seemed like Stefano was actually listening this time. It irritated Sienna that her words and opinions were only valuable to her father when reiterated by a man. But she could live with the unfairness of the double-standard if it meant her father finally accepted her abilities and she achieved her objectives.

King Stephano rejoined his wife and daughter. Axel followed a step behind him and caught Sienna's eye over Stefano's shoulder. He winked at her. Sienna gave him a subtle smile in return. Funny, after resenting Axel for so long, he was turning out to be someone she would like as a friend.

"Are you sure about this, Carissa? And you, Axel?" the king asked. They both nodded in confirmation. King Stefano sighed and suddenly looked much older. "Well, we can't have a wedding where both participants are unwilling. You have my consent. The engagement is dissolved."

"Stefano!" Queen Carmen protested ineffectually.

"Thank you, Papa!" Sienna hugged her father in jubilation and kissed her mother's cheek.

"Well, if you are not getting married, what *are* you going to do?" Sienna wasn't sure if her mother was curious or criticizing.

"I'm going to travel. I want to see places, and not just from the window of the royal coach." She needed to go in search of Aurora. She didn't know where to start but, hopefully, Aurora had gotten their letter and would have some information to share when they entered Dreamworld tonight. As soon as she thought of Dreamworld, a wave of exhaustion hit her. The adrenaline that had propelled her through the day finally faded, leaving her feeling wrung out. She said her goodnights and escaped to the solitary sanctuary of her bedroom. But despite her fatigue, she couldn't keep the smile from her face. She had finally achieved her dual goals of self-defense and self-determination. She was free to follow her own path at last. Nothing could top this feeling.

"Looks like I'm going to Behr!" Sienna announced when she woke up, giddy at the thought that she was free to go where she wanted, and that her parents would no longer try to curtail her.

"What's that, milady?" Sienna hadn't realized that Emmaline was in the room.

"Oh, just saying that I'm going to Behr shortly."

"To see Princess Violetta and your new nephew? How lovely!" Actually, Sienna hadn't considered that, but now she thought about it she would love the chance to see Violetta again, and her home in Behr would be a great base from which to explore the region. She spent her morning in a flurry of organization, chartering a ship and crew to transport her to Behr and ordering supplies to bring with her. Her parents seemed relieved that she was going to visit her sensible older sister, and Sienna saw no need to worry them by mentioning curses, Dreamworlds, or two missing princesses.

She was interrupted by the arrival of the Maester of the Castle, looking flustered. "Excuse me, Your Highness, but you have a visitor. He's waiting in the Rose Salon."

"Who is it, Maester?"

"Prince Sebastian of Vitalia."

24

Sebastian was still sitting in the salon an hour later. He wasn't sure why he had remained there. Still numb from the shock, he guessed. And it wasn't like he had anywhere more pressing to be right now anyway. He didn't know if he was a fool to have asked to see Sienna when everything he wanted to say to her must now be left unsaid for propriety's sake. He just knew that he couldn't leave when he was this close to her without seeing her once more and trying to salvage their friendship at least, even if everything else he had hoped for was now out of reach.

The salon door swung open and he leaped to his feet. Sienna glided in wearing a magnificent gown embroidered with small crystals and a tiara woven into her hair. He had gotten so used to seeing her in more casual day-clothes that it was a sucker-punch to the gut all over again to see her in her royal finery. No one looking at her now would think her a child. She was every inch the sophisticated wife.

"Princess Sienna," he greeted her, bowing as was appropriate to her rank, though more deeply than he should have given their relative positions. He felt the mark of respect was the least he owed her. She responded in kind with a flawlessly executed deep curtsey, exactly the kind she had never bothered to honor him with when she lived at Port Royale.

"Prince Sebastian." He winced at her cool tone and the use of his title. Clearly, he was not forgiven.

"I'm sorry, should I address you as Lady Forrester now?" The name stuck in his throat, but he was determined to be civil about her marriage to that pompous jerk.

Her lips quirked up in that simple smirk of hers. "I am thankful to say that is one name I shall never have to answer to." She obviously read the confusion on his face because she relented and added, "I didn't marry Lord Forrester. I challenged him to a duel instead and proved I don't need his protection. We dissolved our engagement by mutual consent that evening."

The relief coursing through Sebastian was so overwhelming that it was making him dizzy. "I am so glad you didn't marry that pompous jerk!" *Oops, so much for civility.* "Seeing as you are still unattached, I propose that we should get married. We could be on our way back to Port Royale by nightfall."

"Thank you, but no," Sienna replied politely but distantly as if he were an unknown server who had offered her a drink at a soirée. "After the duel, my father has finally accepted that I am capable of defending myself and that he was wrong to try to force me into an unwanted marriage. Thus I no longer need a husband as a smokescreen to hide my actions and true desires."

"Does that mean that you are returning to Port Royale with me, to re-join the Rangers? I have been looking at opening recruitment for more female Rangers and could use your insights."

"I'm not going back to Port Royale," Sienna replied dismissively. "You will have to look elsewhere for your fake bride, as you already turned *my* offer down. Though from the sounds of it you won't have a shortage of candidates to choose from. I won't be training anymore because I have a quest to fulfill and a friend depending on me to succeed."

"Then let me come with you on your quest," Sebastian begged desperately. He was running out of options. She was shutting him out of her life and he couldn't bear it. She looked genuinely surprised by his request and he saw the indifferent façade crack slightly and just a sliver of the mischievous girl who had filled his home with laughter and possibilities peaked through. Sebastian pressed his momentary advantage, knowing that he had to lay it all on the line now or lose her forever.

"Let me come with you. Where you go I'll follow, because I'm only happy when I'm with you and I'm miserable without you. I've told Philippe to stop sending me potential brides because I have already found the only woman I want to marry, and that's *you*, Carissa. I love you. I love you and I just want to be with you – in whatever capacity you will allow me – in the hope that one day I can convince you to marry me and love me too, scars and all."

He unfastened his cloak and deliberately threw it to the ground. He wore no mask underneath. He looked straight at her, not attempting to hide his scars. He could not ask for her acceptance and keep things hidden from her. It was the biggest risk of his life. He had to offer her everything, and just hope that it was enough.

Sienna stared back at him. She didn't flinch away or avert her eyes, but she didn't say anything either. She just stared at him. He could see some emotion swirling in her eyes, but she had gotten too good at schooling her features and he could no longer read her expressions. The longer the silence stretched, the heavier his heart became. But he resolved to stay there until he heard the rejection explicitly from her lips. Even if it shredded his pride, he would not leave wondering 'what if.' He owed it to himself to wait and know if there was any possibility of a 'them' in the future.

SIENNA STARED AT HIM, her mind racing. She was transfixed by his scars. Not because they were ugly, because they weren't, not to her. They were a symbol of the trust he placed in her, by revealing this most intimate part of him. That, more than anything, convinced her of his sincerity. She closed the distance between them and trailed her fingers across his scarred cheek in a gentle caress. She was intoxicated by the knowledge that he was giving her, *her*, the right to touch him like this. She smiled tentatively at him as he leaned into her caress and closed his eyes, enthralled. She watched the peace that spread across his face and gave him the only answer she could, the only truth she had.

"Sounds perfect to me," she whispered. She stood on tiptoe and shyly pressed her lips against his. His eyes snapped open in surprise. He scanned her face, but whatever he saw must have reassured him, because he broke into a luminous smile and pulled her into another embrace. There was nothing shy about this kiss, nothing tentative or unsure. It was the kiss of a man staking his claim where he knew it was welcomed. It demanded and it took and yet it gave and it soothed too. Sienna's head was swimming. She was delirious from the happiness bubbling under her skin, or perhaps from the lack of oxygen. She was so dazed that it took her a moment when Sebastian stopped to realize that he had done so because there was someone else in the room.

"Why are you kissing my sister?" he demanded imperiously.

"Go away Luca," Sienna muttered into Sebastian's shoulder, embarrassed at being caught by her younger brother.

"I am kissing your sister because I intend to marry her," Sebastian told the fifteen-year-old future King of Orella.

"Why does your face look like that? Did you lose a fight?"

"Luca!"

"My face is scarred because I was cursed by a witch. And I rarely lose fights," Sebastian answered patiently.

"Why do you have a red cloak? Are you one of the Red Hoods?"

"I'm actually the leader of the Red Hoods," Sebastian replied. Luca's eyes widened in admiration and Sebastian added, "And your sister is a Red Hood herself."

"Wow, really? So where's her red cloak?"

"Right here," Sebastian said, pulling it out of his bag. "She left without it and I had to return it to her. Once a Ranger, always a Ranger." Sienna had tears in her eyes as she accepted the most iconic part of the Ranger uniform from Sebastian. He was the most wonderful, impossible man, and he loved *her*. She felt like her heart might burst out of her chest from happiness.

"Very well, then," Luca concluded. "I give you my permission to marry my sister. I like this one Si," he said *sotto voce* to her before leaving the room.

"While I am pleased to have secured your brother's permission," Sebastian said to Sienna with a smirk once they were alone again. "The only person whose permission I need is yours." He went down on one knee and looked at her solemnly as he asked her.

"Princess Sienna Nicoletta Antonella Ekaterina di Orella, mia Carissa, will you do me the great honor of marrying me?"

"No."

. . .

Sebastian's face crumpled as he absorbed the shock of her refusal. With no hood or mask to hide behind, Sienna saw every emotion play across his face. She fell to her knees to bring her face level with his and grasped it in both hands, forcing him to look at her.

"You misunderstand me, Sebastian. It's not you I'm refusing, it's marriage. I got a taste of independence during my time in Port Royale, and I don't want to give that up just yet. Marriage ties you down, and I have things I need to do first."

"I don't want to tie you down, Sienna, or limit who you can be."

"But when you marry the court will demand an heir within a year, and I'm not ready for that yet."

"I will wait for you."

"You would?"

"Sienna, I told you *in whatever capacity you will allow*. Just please, tell me whether there is hope, or if I am waiting in vain?"

Sienna kissed him then broke away to embrace him tightly. "Not in vain," she whispered into his shoulder. "I cannot think of anyone in the world I would rather marry. I love you, Sebastian."

"You love me?" he repeated in wonder. "Even though I'm a scarred old man?"

"Oh Sebastian." She sighed exasperatedly. "I've been half in love with you since I was fourteen! I read your books and fell in love with your mind long before I ever saw your face. It never mattered to me what you looked like; that only mattered to you. I see you, all of you, and you are perfect to me."

"And I see you, Sienna. And though you are undeniably beautiful, beauty is the least of your recommendations. You are courageous, loyal, resilient, clever, playful... being beautiful as well is an abundance of riches. And someday, I hope I can also say that you are mine."

"I could never belong to someone unless they belong to me in return."

"Carissa, I'm already yours."

"Then be my partner, my confidante, my companion on my rescue mission. I have a promise to keep."

"Gladly. Who are we rescuing?"

"Princess Aurora von Northaven. Her parents are keeping the news suppressed for now, but she disappeared at the time her curse took effect. No one knows where she is, and we are the only ones who can contact her."

"We?"

"We who share her dreams; the League of Princesses."

The what? Sebastian shook his head and smiled. "There is so much you will have to tell me while we're on our adventure. Before we go, though, there is one thing I would like to clarify between us. I understand and respect your decision not to accept my proposal *at this time*, but I fully intend to marry you one day. So let this be my formal declaration of courtship because I have no intention of abstaining from kissing you until that day."

He pulled her to her feet and into his arms and kissed her until they were both breathless. Sienna broke away, panting and wide-eyed. "I'm glad to hear it," she gasped. "Else 'one day' might have to be a lot sooner than I had planned."

Sebastian groaned. "You encourage me to withhold my kisses as a bargaining chip, but I can't do it. I'm already addicted to yours." He swooped in and kissed her again, swallowing her laughter and sharing it.

So this is what happy feels like, he thought, as he held Sienna curled up against him and knew that regardless of what label they put on it, they were in this together for the rest of their lives. He had found the right woman, one who could see past his flawed exterior to the man he used to be and now was again.

And secure in that knowledge, the last of the scars on his heart finally healed.

EPILOGUE

Sienna stood in Aurora's room staring at the painting on the easel. The image had become clearer over the past few nights, as Aurora added a little more to it each day. There were other such paintings beside other windows around the castle, as Aurora tried to convey to the League what she could see from each window during the daytime. None of the princesses recognized the exact locations – there were no discernable landmarks in any of the views to tie it down. But Izabella thought the contours of the land were reminiscent of those in northern Hessenberg and Selena agreed, which was why Sienna had chosen the province of Behr as the starting point for her search.

"There you are!" Natashya bounded into the room but cocked her head at Sienna when she turned around. "You look different to last night, like you're lit up inside. What's going on?"

"Can't I just be excited that I'm finally going on my first quest?"

"You could be, but this is something else. What is it?"

Sienna laughed. She couldn't hide something this big from her best friend for long. They sat by the fireplace as the whole story tumbled out, from the appearance of a disheveled Sebastian in her home that afternoon to the sneaky kiss he claimed just before bedtime.

"And he's going with you to help rescue Aurora?"

"Yes, we leave together in the morning. What about you? How is your quest going?"

Natashya sighed. "Well, I met Odette today but she didn't seem herself."

"How so?"

"Lots of little things. Any one alone I could dismiss, but all together? It's making my skin prickle like when there's a blizzard coming in. Alexei thinks I'm overreacting, but I think *he's* being naïve. He came with me because he is hoping to create an alliance between Siverus and Bretonnia, and doesn't want to consider anything that might put that idea in jeopardy."

"Alexei and Odette?"

Natashya shrugged. "Maybe? They got on well when she came to stay with us that summer."

"Tell me about Odette."

Sienna listened to all of Natashya's observations, and her own concern increased with each one. Natashya was right; something was very wrong.

"I need to get to Lord Avigny's chateau. If Odette is living there, there has to be an opportunity to talk alone before bedtime, or early in the morning. I still don't know how she avoids coming to Dreamworld each night."

Sienna sympathized with her friend's frustration but didn't see how transferring to the home of Odette's guardian and Regent would help. If there was a deliberate effort to prevent private conversation between her and Odette, it would continue regardless of location. A princess stood out too much to be stealthy, and she said as much.

Natashya's shoulders slumped at the reminder, but then

she sat up straight, a new light in her eyes. "What if it isn't a Princess who goes to Chateau Avigny, but a servant? Princess Natashya would be conspicuous, but no one would notice the new serving girl Asha! They won't be guarding against a servant – and servants often have a lot more access and knowledge of their masters' affairs than is prudent."

"That's a drastic step, Ash," Sienna cautioned. "Are you sure about this?"

"Yes."

"Okay then. How will you get hired?" If her best friend was embarking on a risky quest, Sienna would make sure that she had a plan for every contingency, to protect her as much as possible. The princesses turned their discussion to practicalities and logistics. The fire had burned low by the time Sienna was satisfied they had covered everything. Asha looked daunted but determined, and Sienna felt a swell of pride in her friend.

"I know you'll get to the bottom of the mystery and if Odette needs help, I can't think of a better champion for her than you, Asha."

"Thanks, Sienna. Coming from you, that really means a lot to me. And I know with you on the ground acting on the information we gather here in Dreamworld, Aurora's curse will be broken in no time."

"And we'll all help with Odette too, as soon as you can tell us what we are dealing with. You and I can exchange notes on our quests each night before we sleep. One advantage of Dreamworld is that it is the most secure communication network I can think of. No risk of eavesdroppers or correspondence tampering here!"

Natashya laughed. "Trust you to find the tactical bright side! We will get our girls back because we made a promise to each other four years ago: to believe in ourselves and not rely on a prince to save us. You showed us that was possible, and made us a team. Now, the team has come together to help two of our own, and that's how I know we will succeed."

Sienna smiled with the certainty of success. "Yes, we will."

~

SIENNA WAS STILL SMILING when she woke up. Her attendant Emmaline had laid out a pale-yellow traveling dress and matching bonnet on the chaise, ready for her to get dressed. Sienna pondered the choice for a moment but decided that if she was going to break expectations that others had of her, she was going to break them all. She picked a different outfit, one that was far more comfortable and suited to the task at hand. She had commissioned it after her duel with Axel, though she had approached the seamstress directly in secret because she knew her mother would disapprove and didn't want to waste time arguing. She paused for a moment when she finished dressing to admire her new look in the mirror. She picked up her red hooded cloak and held it close, to savor the thrill that it was really hers, before fastening it around her. Feeling elated at her new status, she headed down the stairs to the entrance hall.

She heard the voices before she turned the corner on the staircase and became visible to the men talking below. She stopped when she realized they were talking about *her*. Should she continue down and interrupt their conversation, or wait to hear what they were saying? She had just decided to continue when she heard something that made her heart freeze in her chest.

"This trip seems to be something Sienna feels strongly about, so of course, I can't stop her going," King Stefano was saying. "But I must say how relieved I am that you are accompanying her. You will protect her, won't you?"

"I think you have misunderstood my role here, Your Majesty. Your daughter does not need me to stand between her and danger. She is highly capable of protecting herself. But I will stand by her side for as long as she will have me, as a supporter not a savior, her partner not her protector."

Her heart thawed and started to soar, pounding an excited rhythm in her chest. Who cared if her father still thought her a child in need of guarding, despite everything she had done? Sebastian believed in her. She believed in herself too. She knew she could do this without him. She *could*, but she didn't have to, because he was with her. Not because she needed him to be there, but because they both *wanted* to be there together. Happiness bubbled up inside her again and again and a smile lit up her face as she turned on the staircase and strolled down the final leg to join the two most important men in her life.

SEBASTIAN LOOKED up when he heard the tread on the stair and almost swallowed his tongue when he saw what Sienna was wearing. She had discarded her court dresses in favor of traveling clothes similar to what he or the other Rangers would wear, but there was nothing masculine about her appearance. The leathers that served as lightweight armor were tailored to her figure in a way that was simultaneously practical and alluring. He was suddenly extremely conscious of her father's watchful eye beside him, and he silently cursed the propriety that prevented him from sweeping her into his arms and kissing her until she was breathless, as he wanted to do. Something must have shown on his face though; he was still adjusting to his face being visible rather than hidden in his hood as it used to be. Sienna's smile got impossibly wider and her eyes gained a mischievous twinkle. She walked right up to him and kissed him on the cheek, ignoring their audience. She kissed him on his *scarred* cheek, and her complete acceptance undid him.

"Hey," he croaked, his mouth suddenly dry.

"Hey," she replied softly, with a smile just for him. A discreet cough from King Stefano broke the spell and she turned her attention to taking her leave of her family, the rest of whom had just joined them. While she said farewell to Prince Luca, who was pawing at her red cloak in admiration, Axel Forrester entered the hall. Sebastian came to full alert, ready to step in if he did anything to upset Sienna, but Forrester came directly to him.

"Be good to her. She deserves it."

"I know. I will be."

Forrester paused, as if to weigh Sebastian's words, then nodded decisively in acceptance. He offered his hand, and Sebastian shook it, giving him a nod in return. There was nothing more they needed to say to each other. Forrester went to say goodbye to Sienna, and Sebastian tamped down the urge to hit him just for talking to her. But Sienna was soon at his side, and thoughts of doing violence to foreign aristocrats quickly faded. They walked to the courtyard together and Sebastian held her horse's reins while she mounted, checked the saddlebags were secure, then mounted his own horse. He looked across at her.

"Are you sure you want to come?" she asked nervously.

"Where you go, I go," he answered simply.

She smiled. "Then let's go rescue a princess!"

They spurred their horses and rode through the palace gates and into their future, side by side.

~ The End ~

~

Something is rotten in the kingdom of Bretonnia...

Join Princess Natashya as she goes undercover as the serving girl Asha in a bid to find out what happened to her friend Princess Odette. *The Frog Prince*, *Cinderella*, and *Swan Lake* collide, in the next book in the series:

The Golden Ball
https://books2read.com/TheGoldenBall

Turn the page for a preview of Chapter 1.

AUTHOR NOTES

Thank you!

Thank you for reading my book, and for sticking around to read my notes and to let me say hello to you. I hope you enjoyed Sienna and Sebastian's story. It is three years since I first started writing it, in October 2017. That was based on an idea I first started in February 2015. What if Beauty from Beauty and the Beast was also Little Red Riding Hood? That premise created a parallel between the Beast and the Wolf, and once I had the Big Bad Wolf, I had to include the Three Little Pigs too, and the story grew from there.

So, then I put the project away for a while.

Yes, you read that correctly. No, I don't recommend this approach to writing! Three scenes and an epilogue from the finish, I went off to chase another project instead. But the following May my father went to hospital for surgery, and he never came home. He died in June 2018. My parents have always been supportive of me. While parts of Sienna are like me, the lack of understanding her parents showed toward her is definitely fiction, and I am thankful for that every day. This book is dedicated to Dad because his death was a catalyst for me to stop wasting my time on another story I wasn't enjoying, and come back and finish this one.

As I write this, *The Golden Ball* (book 2) is drafted and with my second beta team, and *The Princess Vow* (book 3) is about halfway written. But if you want a little more from Fable while you wait, how about the story of how Sebastian's brother Philippe met his future queen Marianne? *The Orphan Queen* is a mashup of The Ugly Duckling and Cinderella, with a dash of Sherlock Holmes mystery. It's for sale on Amazon, but you can get it for free when you sign up to my newsletter. So if you want new releases, cover reveals, news, and updates before anyone else (and another visit to Fable) you can join here: https://www.subscribepage.com/erika-everest-scarred-prince.

A special thanks to my own Prince Charming and our beautiful royal-minis. Your love and support make me feel like I can do anything, even something as scary as publish a book! When I get lost in my imaginary worlds, you are the beacon that guides me home. Thank you.

Collectively, my Jitterbugs are the best combination beta and proofreading team a girl could ask for! Jim, Kelly, Sarah, Micky, and Nat – you were my first readers and gave me the hope that I wasn't wasting my time on this idea. Special thanks to Jim who has continued to demand updates, and not let me slack off from my writing since! Another thanks to Abie Williams and Celestine Caplan, two wonderful teenagers who read an early draft of my book to assess the appeal to a YA audience. Angela, Arielle, Robyn, Laura, and Coralie, my fabulous fairytale friends, thank you for your genre-specific insights and all your support in the last year. And Dorothy, thanks for stepping in to do a final proofing pass to catch any errant typos. Any errors remaining are entirely my own. If you spot any errors, typos, or unicorns, please let me know! You can reach me at Erika@erikaeverest.com, and I'd welcome your feedback. Especially about the unicorns.

You can also find me on Facebook in the Fairytale Courtyard reader group (https://www.facebook.com/groups/FairytaleCourtyard) or at my author page (https://www.facebook.com/ErikaEverestAuthor).

Turn the page for a sneak peek at book two in the *Tales from the Kingdoms of Fable* series: *The Golden Ball*.

Happy (ever after) reading!

Erika.

10th October 2020

THE GOLDEN BALL

Unflappable, untouchable, serene, Princess Alexandrina Natashya Siverusova stood at the prow of the ship while the crew scurried around her. The chaos surrounding her could not penetrate her aura of solitude. That aura had developed over years of carefully controlling and concealing her emotions. She knew the courtiers called her the Ice Princess, but she embraced the title. As Tsarevna of Siverus, she was the heir to the second most powerful kingdom in Fable. Her people expected her to rule dispassionately, without favoritism or personal bias. She expected it of herself. She constantly strove to be 'perfect' so her conduct would always be above reproach, but it was hard to form friendships under those constraints.

No, that was just an excuse.

The truth was that she wasn't good with people. She didn't understand them, couldn't read them, as bitter experience had taught her. The memory of Dmitri's betrayal still made her cringe inside. She had been so gullible, so naïve, but no more. She wasn't that girl any longer. She had cultivated her protective shell and mastered the art of being amiable without inviting familiarity, of appearing engaged without letting herself become emotionally invested. It was a fine line to walk, and exhausting too, but that was the price being a princess demanded.

"Weigh anchor!" The Captain's order reverberated around the deck and the crew rushed to comply.

"Anchors aweigh!"

Natashya always savored the moment the wind filled the sails and the ship lifted into the air. As they took flight, the swooping sensation in her stomach made exhilaration bubble up inside her. Her spirits rose with the great vessel, and for a brief moment the responsibilities that weighed on her lifted too, allowing her to see the possibilities of the world rather than the problems. That moment of weightlessness sustained her when reality intruded again. She watched with a pang of trepidation as the castle that was her home grew smaller beneath her, shading her eyes against the glare of the sunlight on the white snow below.

"And away we go," a voice murmured beside her. She didn't need to turn around; she knew the voice as well as her own. Beside her, her twin brother lounged against the prow. She glanced at him. They had the same startlingly pale blue eyes and the same white-blond hair. But while Asha's hair was always perfectly pinned and styled, Alexei's usually looked mussed up, as if he had just rolled out of bed and couldn't be bothered combing it. Actually, come to think of it, that was pretty much how he achieved the look each day. She thought he was too sloppy and casual for a Tsarevich and needed to learn to take life more seriously. He thought she was too uptight and logical and needed to have some more fun in her life. But woe betide any external party foolish enough to voice similar thoughts to either of them, because they loved each other fiercely and neither permitted criticism of the other from outsiders.

When the ship rose high enough through the clouds

that there was nothing left to see, they went below deck to lunch.

"When will we get to Bretonnia?"

Asha looked hard at Alexei. Something was up with him; he *knew* how long the journey took. "As long as this good wind stays with us, a little less than three days to the Bretonnian coast, and then half a day's ride by coach to reach the capital," she answered anyway.

"Hmm. Do you think Princess Odette will have changed much since we last saw her?"

"She was thirteen when she came to stay with us, and is about to turn sixteen. Women tend to change a lot in that time, so yes." There was a slight bite in Asha's words, a tonal shading she would never let any but her closest circle hear. Her façade of icy perfection was her mask and her armor. She didn't have the social tools her brothers were blessed with, and all her studying could only compensate so much. She had learned the hard way that being open and approachable often meant being approached by the wrong people, and she lacked the social sensors to identify their ill intent. With as much power as she wielded as the heir to Siverus, she found it safer to keep everyone distant rather than risk letting anyone close again who might try to use her.

Alexei heard the bite and abandoned his attempts at nonchalance. "Have you heard from Odette recently? Do you have any reason to believe there might be something wrong?"

Asha looked at him sharply. *What did he know? And how?* "Alexei?"

That was all she said. Just his name. But the imperious querying tone was so reminiscent of their mother it made him wince.

"Well, you see, after Odette came to stay with us, she and

I kept in touch. We wrote to each other every few weeks, but my last three letters have gone unanswered. I haven't heard from her in months."

Asha just stared at him, shock wiping away her usual blank expression.

"Are you out of your mind?" she hissed. "I would expect that sort of behavior from Jack but not from *you*, Alexei. I thought you were my sensible brother! Do you have any idea of the potential diplomatic incident such correspondence could cause if it ever came to light? It would be the scandal of the century! And of course, it's Odette that would suffer the brunt of it – the snide remarks, the lewd expectations, the complete destruction of her reputation... Women always come out worse in those scenarios. *You* would probably get a pat on the back from the old boys club!"

"Sis, are you okay? I've never seen you so agitated. Calm down, we were careful. Odette has a servant she trusts and she helped us keep the correspondence secret."

"Oh, this gets better and better. You had a *secret* correspondence with another kingdom's princess? You do realize that you were essentially courting Odette with those letters, right?"

"What's wrong with that?" he asked defensively.

"You *intended* to court her?"

"I like her, Asha. She's smart and funny, and despite everything she's been through she can still find joy in the little things around her."

"And yet, while courting this princess you claim to like, you were still having liaisons back at court. How do you think Odette would feel if she knew about you and Count Pavlov's wife?"

"Elisaveta was bored because Pavlov is too old to appreciate her how she wants to be appreciated. But she is already married. Though we have been, um, close, she wouldn't stand in the way of my own marriage or happiness."

"Can you say the same for Katya Chekhov, the Minister for the Treasury's daughter?"

Alexei turned bright red. "How do you even know about her?" he stammered.

"Brother dearest, you are not nearly as discreet as you think you are. That girl has talked far more than she should."

Alexei shrugged. "Katya and I had a good time, but it was nothing serious. She knows that. Neither Katya nor Elisaveta have any impact on my relationship with Odette. It was just a bit of fun. You should try it sometime."

Natashya stared at him perplexed. For a smart boy, he really could be very dense at times. Did he truly have no idea of the double standards that existed in how the behaviors of men and women were judged? He might be able to shrug off his affairs as unimportant, but she wondered if his paramours would share his view. Elisaveta Pavlova was mature enough to understand the game. While she might miss the young and handsome distraction from her dour older husband, she would have had no long-term expectations of Alexei. Not so Katya Chekhov. The poor girl seemed to think that Alexei was going to make her his princess. Natashya hadn't worked out yet if she was just naïvely foolish in dreaming of her handsome prince, or if she was actually a manipulative social climber trying to use her dalliance with the Prince to elevate her from the plebian classes. Either way, she would be disappointed. The Tsarevich was not one to be coerced or guilted into marriage. His reputation would suffer nothing for the affair; Katya was only damaging her own prospects by continuing to talk about it as indiscriminately as she had.

Somedays Natashya wished she could just ignore her

responsibilities and have 'a bit of fun' like Alexei so glibly suggested, but she had never met anyone for whom she was willing to risk her reputation, her marriage prospects, and her throne. She had too much at stake, and everyone had an angle they were playing. It was why she was certain that falling in love would not be part of her future. She just couldn't imagine letting her guard down long enough to develop that much trust in someone. She knew that she would marry, because she would need an heir someday. She expected that, when she felt ready for that step, she would discuss it with her parents and identify a prince from one of the other kingdoms not in the direct line of succession, so there would be no conflict of interest with her sovereignty of Siverus. Maybe Prince Henry from Anglia or Prince Christian from Karjala. She hoped that she could come to like and respect her husband after their marriage, but that was the most she *could* hope for. She was aware of her limitations, and the emotional capacity to love without regard for consequences was something that eluded her. No, she was resigned to it.

Falling in love was not for her.

https://books2read.com/TheGoldenBall

ALSO BY ERIKA EVEREST

Tales from the Kingdoms of Fable

The Scarred Prince – October 2020

The Golden Ball – December 2020

The Princess Vow – Spring 2021

The Rebellious Royal – Coming 2022

Made in the USA
Monee, IL
06 December 2024